Gwen

K.N. BAKER

House of Honor Books

House of Honor

ISBN: 978-1-68596-083-4

Printed in the United States of America

Published by House of Honor Books.

Harvest, Alabama

In loving memory of

Snow's Majesty and Nancy Baker

In dedication to

my friends and family at Family Medicine Specialists,
my poetry professor Michael Latza,
Jillian Narayan,
my supportive and inspiring father

INTRODUCTION

Gwen's life was dull and uninspiring. She went to bed at nine thirty every night and woke up at five thirty every morning. She was a boring girl. Although she was no longer a girl, she was a middle-aged, divorced woman.

Bitter and easily annoyed often giving heavy sighs of contempt in her daily life. She was stuck in a routine. Then again, where was a forty-year-old woman to go. She lived in a neighborhood a few streets behind a busy highway with her cat named Snow. Her home was small but cozy, slate blue with navy shutters, simple and nothing more than ordinary. She came to accept that her life was as good as it was going to get.

One day she decided to drive past her childhood home out in the country. It had a charming white porch. Her swing still swayed from the old oak tree in the front yard. Gwen parked by the mailbox. She got out and walked up the asphalt driveway where a red pickup truck sat. The same scalloped valances her mother hung in the windows were still there. She went up the steps and rang the bell. An old lady with short curly hair opened the door.

"Hi, I'm sorry to bother you. This was my childhood home. I don't know why but I was thinking about it. I wanted to come see it again. Is it okay if I come in?" Gwen asked.

"Of course, please, come in," the lady said, holding the door open for her.

"It's just like I remember," Gwen said.

"We haven't changed much," the lady replied.

1

"Please, have a seat."

The tea kettle whistled in the kitchen.

"Would you like some tea?" the old woman offered.

"No thank you, I don't want to be a bother," Gwen said.

"Oh, no bother. How about something to eat? Do you like blueberry scones?"

"No thanks, I'm not really hungry," Gwen politely declined.

"Suit yourself, I'll be right back," the woman told her as she reached for a cane and wobbled off to the kitchen

"If it's okay, may I see my room?" Gwen called to the old woman.

"Please, go right ahead."

Gwen walked down a short hallway to her old bedroom. It had been turned into a guest room. Her pink walls had been painted white. A twin bed was pushed against the wall in front of the window. Opening the closet she saw a cardboard box on the shelf.

Gwen placed the box on the bed and opened it to find an emerald book. She picked it up and opened it. The pages were filled with words. Curious she closed it, looking for the title.

"What?" She muttered.

As she opened the book back up, the pages were blank. She flipped the first few pages looking for a title but there was none. She went faster through more pages.

I could have sworn the pages were full.

In a flash of memory, it came back to her. Her mother would read to her from the book at bedtime.

"This is mom's book," she said frazzled.

Suddenly, the pages began to glow. She watched as letters written in gold appeared on the plain cover to spell out, *Gwen*. There was a knock on the door and the letters disappeared into the cover.

"What's going on in there?" the old woman asked, stepping into the room. "It's getting late. I think it's time for you to go."

"Yes, of course. Before I go, I found something. This was my mother's book. She always read it to me when I was little. May I keep it?" Gwen asked.

The woman looked at the box on the bed and nodded. "Yes, you may keep it, dear."

When she arrived back home, Gwen put the book on the coffee table. Snow jumped onto the table sniffing at the newfound treasure.

"What do you think about the book Snow?" Gwen asked.

He placed one paw on top of the cover and started to purr. Suddenly, he jumped from the table and ran out the front door that Gwen had forgotten to close.

"Snow! Come back! Where are you going?" She called as she ran after him.

In the house, the title returned in glimmering gold. The book flew open, and the pages began to fill with words as if it was writing its own story.

CHAPTER 1

SIR JERICHO'S KINGDOM

Gwen ran out into the street, looking in both directions for Snow. Not seeing him, she ran further and further. Unseen behind her, the windows of the house slammed shut. Behind the windows, the curtains waved on an unseen wind and the book continued to write itself. Each page the book wrote ripped itself free. As pages flew out, newly written words appeared ever faster. When the very last page reached the floor, the book closed. A small flame ignited on the cover, burning the name *Gwen* onto it. Orange embers flickered there until the fire extinguished itself and small bits of ash floated around.

"Snow!" Gwen called for her kitty, passing along a street of suburban houses.

She went around the corner sprinting over a rippling creek and rushed into the woods as the wind shimmied the autumn leaves.

"Snoooow!" she cried, hurrying over broken tree branches.

It was harvest time and acorns lay scattered on the ground. The sky was a cool blue. It was the middle of October and deep in the woods was the first frost. In the distance, she saw a fluffy white tail.

"Snow," she gasped as she ran to catch up to him.

His tail disappeared behind a bush, and she followed pushing her way through. On the other side lay a forest path where Snow stopped and sat watching her with his glowing blue eyes.

"There you are," she said relieved, picking him up as he purred. "Why did you run off like that?"

He continued purring as he looked at the path before them.

"Let's go back home. I'm sure you're hungry," she said.

Gwen turned around and noticed the season had changed. It was no longer chilly. There were no leaves on the ground and the trees were alive with greenery. Sunbeams twinkled through the branches illuminating the shimmering path.

"We'll just go back the way we came," she told Snow.

She turned around looking for the bush but saw only a long winding path. It swerved down and around the forest going on for miles. The trees were tall and thick, their leaves hanging over the dirt road, their shadows dancing on the ground.

"It's here somewhere. I think maybe it's over here," she said and started walking looking at the shrubs as she went.

"Maybe it's this one."

Gwen held Snow in her left arm as she pushed through the bush. As she walked through, everything turned dark. She reached out and her arm started to slowly disappear. She gasped, quickly drawing it back and cautiously reached out again. As she did, her hand became invisible, and everything was pitch black.

"Oh no! How are we going to get home?" her voice filled with panic as Snow's purrs vibrated louder.

She walked backward out of the darkness returning to the path. She turned around and heard the birds chirping and flying high above her.

"We're gonna get out of here somehow. Where did you bring us?" she asked Snow.

She looked around as a squirrel ran up the trunk

of an oak tree. Crickets sang, and dragonflies buzzed over small white and purple flowers in the grass. The fresh air blew against her face. She tucked her hair behind her ear and walked on. In the warm day, she started sweating. Wiping her forehead, she placed Snow on the ground and pulled her sweater over her head revealing a brown t-shirt underneath. She took the sweater and tied it around her waist.

Things all looked very peculiar. The forest was unlike any she had ever seen. There were bleeding hearts and iridescent moon flowers in the shade. The air smelled of fresh pine and rose petals. There were shrubs of gardenias.

"Oh Snow, it's like we found another country. How will we ever get back home?" she asked.

She walked for an hour before looking for a good place to sit down to rest. Snow jumped up next to her wiping his face and licking his paws.

"Are your paws dirty?" Gwen asked, using the sleeve of her sweater to clean him.

Her phone started ringing as she reached into her pocket.

"At least I have my phone." She raised her eyebrows; it was her boss. "Hello?"

"Gwen?" he asked, his voice muffled by static.

"Hello?" she said covering her other ear.

"Gwen, where are you? Your vacation ended yesterday and you're not here," he shouted through the white noise.

"I'm lost! I don't know where I am," she said, stress taking over as her ear filled with static. "Hello?"

She pulled her phone away, lifting it up searching for a signal.

"I'll take that," a high-pitched voice said.

A small fairy with brown hair and holographic wings snatched the phone from Gwen's hand.

"Hey! Give that back!" Gwen cried.

The fairy fled and Gwen ran after her. Snow

meowed as he followed behind. The fairy flew around a corner and past a blue wisteria tree. Gwen came to a halt, catching her breath.

"Looking for this?" the fairy asked as she dangled the phone over a wide pond with a flowing waterfall.

"No, please! Don't drop that! I need it!" Gwen's eyes grew wide.

The fairy giggled, releasing it. Gwen tried to catch it but missed and watched as it went under.

"Oh my god. You don't have any idea what you've done," Gwen said grabbing the sides of her head.

"Are you sure about that?" the fairy asked.

"Am I sure about that? Of course, I'm sure about that," Gwen shouted.

"Why don't you take a few steps back." The fairy coughed waving her hand.

"Excuse me, you just stole my phone and destroyed it!" Gwen exclaimed.

"Let me show you something. Then maybe you'll understand. Take a few steps back," the fairy insisted.

Gwen slowly took a few steps and stood next to Snow.

"Look down," the fairy said pointing at the ground.

Gwen's eyebrows furrowed in confusion as she looked.

"Why am I standing on a rainbow?" she asked as Snow looked up at her and began purring.

The fairy covered her mouth giggling. "Look closer," she said.

Gwen knelt down. There *was* a rainbow underneath her. As she leaned closer, she saw it was translucent. She could see the blue sky and clouds moving. Snow tilted his head looking and headbutted her. She scratched his chin. As she was getting up, she saw the entire forest path under the dirt was a rainbow. Wiping the dirt off of her clothes, she looked up at the trees to see if the rainbow was a reflection.

But it wasn't.

"Where am I?" she asked in confusion.

Snow's eyes twinkled glowing.

"You'll find out soon enough," the fairy said.

"Soon enough? Why can't you tell me where I am?" Gwen questioned.

"Well because, you're here. And here is the only place you need to be." The fairy smiled.

"I see. Do you know how I can get out of here? I really need to get home. And it seems I can't go back the way I came," Gwen explained.

"There's no need to worry. None of that matters anymore," the fairy said as she twirled in the air.

"It must be wonderful being a fairy. You seem so carefree." Gwen said.

"Oh, it is. I love being a fairy. And you too can be carefree."

"I don't think I can. You know, being a human and all. I have responsibilities. I can't just leave that all behind," Gwen said.

"Oh, you just don't get it. That's okay, with time you will." The fairy shook her tiny head and sparkles fell from her hair.

"So, what's your name?" Gwen asked.

"I'm Quildorra. Nice to meet you And you are?"

"I'm Gwen and this is Snow," she replied.

"Gwen…" the fairy paused, scratching her chin. "Why does that name ring my bells?" she asked as the sound of fairy bells rang

"Well, it's a common name. There are millions of Gwen's in the world. I'm certain we've never met before. I never even knew fairies existed," Gwen said enthusiastically.

"What? How could you think such a thing. Of course, we exist. If humans exist, and cats, and dogs, and fish, then how come fairies can't exist?" the fairy asked surprised.

"Well, it's just that I've never actually seen one

before," Gwen said.

"Oh, you humans are always missing the magic right in front of you. You can be so oblivious sometimes," Quildorra said exasperated. "It's okay everyone. You can come out now."

She used her fingers to whistle. Echoes of whispers encircled Gwen. Her ears perked up following the sounds.

"We've been expecting you and we're glad you're finally here," Quildorra said as the fairies came out from hiding.

One by one they appeared from behind flowers and shrubs. Their wings chimed as they flew.

"Oh my gosh, it's her," one fairy gasped.

"It can't be," another fairy said in disbelief.

"It has to be her. She has hair of sunshine and eyes of evergreens," a fairy said excitedly.

"It's Gwen. It's Gwen. You guys, it's Gwen!" another fairy cheered.

"What's going on?" Gwen hesitated as she slowly backed away. "How do you all know my name?"

"It's alright. There's no need to be scared," said a fairy with sparkly pink wings who fluttered nearby.

"You must be thirsty," Quildorra said.

"I am. I've been walking for miles," Gwen said.

"Please, drink from the pond," Quildorra suggested.

"Are you sure? Is the water safe?" Gwen asked.

"Yes, of course, it's safe. Why wouldn't it be?" the fairy asked.

Behind Quildorra, the fairies frolicked by the water. They sat on moss-covered stones and flew by the waterfall. Toads leaped from lily pads where blush lotuses floated.

"Well okay. I am very thirsty," Gwen said as she leaned over the pond, cupped the water in her hands and gulped it down. "Mmm, it's so sweet."

The fairies giggled as she quenched her thirst.

Gwen stopped slurping and looked at her hands. The water shimmered in swirls of gold and pink. She watched the elixir slurry with a gasp and opened her hands letting the potion splash into the pond. The surface broke into ripples before returning to blue. Gwen looked at her reflection. Her appearance altered before her eyes. Her skin brightened, her hair softened, and her jade eyes twinkled. She watched as time reversed and she became ten years younger.

"What did you do to me?" she asked, rising to her feet.

She looked at the waterfall and a maiden emerged from the falling waters. Her graceful movements carried her on the water toward Gwen until she stepped barefoot onto the grass. She was magnificent, like a guardian or a spirit. She had long and smooth platinum hair that swayed below her hips as she walked. Her complexion was fair as snow and without blemish. She was tall and thin with eyes of silver ice. She wore a crown woven from silver twigs and small white flowers. Her sheer, metallic, white silk dress hugged her waist. It was embroidered in silver Celtic designs with long flared sleeves. Her pointed ears peeked through her hair. The sprinkles of water on her skin froze into diamonds.

"I've restored you," the maiden spoke.

"Restored me? I was perfectly happy the way I was. I didn't consent to this," Gwen spoke frustrated.

"Perhaps, but now you are healed. You've been renewed," she said.

"Well maybe I didn't want to be renewed. You could have asked me first."

"We've been expecting you," the maiden told her.

"Expecting me? Why would you expect me? Who are you? What is this place?" Gwen asked, frantic.

"I am Sinnafain, and these are my fairies. Welcome to *Sir Jericho's Kingdom,* and my forest. We expect you'll do great things while you're here," she explained.

"Well, I don't expect to do anything here. I need to get home," Gwen insisted.

"Oh dear, you don't know, do you?" she asked.

"Don't know what? What are you talking about? Everything has been very confusing ever since I got here," Gwen explained.

"I don't suppose you'll ever go back. But if you really want to, I presume you could. You just have to endure the void and walk through the darkness. That is, if it doesn't consume you along the way."

"Consume me? What am I doing here?" Gwen asked.

"There are great things that await you, Gwen," she replied and turned to the cat. "Hello, Snow, have some water.

"Snow, don't drink that!" Gwen cried. "What are you doing to my cat?"

"Now. now, calm down. It'll be alright. He's just thirsty, that's all," Sinnafain said in a soothing voice.

When the cat finished, he licked his mouth and ran back to stand beside Gwen. Sinnafain smiled and magenta geraniums blossomed in the grass around her.

"So why me? Why not pick somebody else?" Gwen asked.

"Because no one has a heart as genuine as yours. You're pure," the maiden said.

"I see," Gwen said.

"The water you drank is a gift I am bestowing upon you," Sinnafain told her.

"A gift? I can't accept a gift. I don't deserve it," Gwen protested.

"Oh, but you do. You deserve it more than anyone," Sinnafain assured her.

"What is this gift?" Gwen asked.

"It is a gift of true love and eternal beauty."

"I'm sorry but you must have mistaken me for someone else. I don't believe in true love. Such a thing doesn't exist," Gwen said and snickered.

Sinnafain's eyes suddenly turned into bright lights that beamed into Gwen's. Unable to move or speak Gwen's body levitated off the ground. Sinnafain delved into her mind and Gwen's pain and despair reflected in her irises. Time stopped as memories opened to her Gwen's grief, heartbreak, and the loss of her parents.

Sinnafain watched as Gwen cried at the docks, sulked in her bed, and watched Daniel slam the door as he left. She listened to his cruel and malicious words. "Leave me alone. Stay out of my life. I never loved you and never will. If I never speak to you again, I think I'll live. You never were or will be my woman. You're beating a dead horse. You're delusional and psycho."

Gwen's heart burned as a hot fuchsia light glowed through the skin of her chest. The aura faded in and out illuminating her ribs. As Sinnafain held Gwen by her shirt continuing to watch, tears filled her eyes. They flooded over as droplets fell down her perfect face. Her eyes poured as she watched their final goodbye.

The streams of Sinnafain's tears froze into icicles. She gestured with her head, lowering Gwen back to the ground and time resumed.

"What did you just do to me?" Gwen asked.

"I took a look to see if you're the Gwen we've been waiting for," she said.

"I told you, I'm not. I can't possibly be."

"Oh, but you are," Sinnafain assured her.

"I really don't think I am. But I'm stuck here and so it doesn't really matter," Gwen stated.

"Hold still for a moment. This will only hurt a little bit," Sinnafain said.

She waved her hand in the air twisting her wrist and a red glowing ball appeared in her palm.

"What is that?" Gwen asked when Sinnafain pushed the sphere forward.

The ball spun and struck Gwen in the chest, knocking her back. It burst into purples and reds. Gwen tried to keep her balance as the ball was immersed inside of her.

"What was that?" Gwen asked touching the top of her chest.

"All will be revealed in time, dear. Follow the fairies," Sinnafain instructed.

Her feet sparkled and silver glitter spiraled around her as she disappeared. The fairies laughed and giggled as they flew over the pond towards Gwen.

"Come Gwen, this way. Follow us," a fairy in front of her said.

The fairy was the darkest shade of black. Her tiny eyes were a bright yellow gold, and her hair was long, and as black as she was. Her wings changed colors whenever she wanted.

"Wow." Gwen looked adoringly at the fairy.

"What is it?" the fairy asked.

"It's just...I've never seen anything so beautiful. Look at you, your skin is black as night and your eyes are so magical. I've never seen a black fairy before. You're stunning."

She giggled. "Oh well thank you. We fairies come in all different colors."

"It's amazing. You're all so exquisite. The universe created you in all its beauty," Gwen said.

"I guess so. I do love colors but inside we're all the same. We all just want to fly and be free!" the fairy exclaimed.

"What's your name?" Gwen asked.

"I'm Shadow." She smiled, flying around releasing golden sparkles.

"It's nice to meet you, Shadow."

Gwen smiled as she and fairies of peach, pink, blue, and purple made their way through the forest.

Their wings were translucent and shimmered. After a while, Snow slowed and laid on the ground.

"Awe he must be tired. Here, let me help," a navy fairy with white iridescent wings said.

She flew over to the cat and sprinkled blue fairy dust over him. He lifted off the ground, floated along and gave a big yawn.

"Ick! Tuna breath," a ruby fairy complained.

Up ahead Gwen saw an opening that led onto a grassy field where bright sunshine greeted her.

"Thanks for showing me the way guys," Gwen said but there was no response all the fairies were gone. "Quildorra? Shadow? Snow, wake up."

The kitty gradually opened its eyes as he sunk to the ground. He yawned when Gwen leaned down to pick him up. As she did, a bird landed in a tree next to her and started pecking the bark. Gwen recognized the woodpecker as the one in her room.

"You!" she exclaimed.

The woodpecker chirped, turning its head to look at her for a moment before it flew off over the grasslands.

"Who brought us here. Whose plan was this?" she pondered aloud.

She stepped out of the forest to feast her eyes on fields far and wide. The blue sky was filled with voluptuous cumulus clouds. The wind smelled of honeysuckle. Surrounded by serenity, Gwen closed her eyes breathing in the fresh air. When she opened them again, she was wearing a chiffon dress. It was a Celtic design like the maiden wore, but mauve and brown. It had two gold silk ribbons that laced across the front tied over in a bow. She looked down at the dress, feeling the material on her body. She lifted the bottom to see she still had her boots on.

"Oh my," she said in surprise. Her breasts were rounder, fuller than before.

It occurred to Gwen that perhaps she was supposed to be here. She no longer felt lost. She now felt as if she had been found. She had never seen a world so vibrant. She ran through the fields and Snow followed, leaping after a pine butterfly. Gwen spread her arms, laughed, and spun around.

In the distance, she saw mountains as tall as the sky, their tops in the clouds. She ran through the fields of gold, swiping her hands through the wheat as their soft tips brushed against her dress. She lay down in the field watching the ginormous clouds drift by and listening to the crashing of waves far away. Her eyes were on the brilliant sky when a dark shadow passed over her.

Giant metallic scales flew over so close she couldn't move, and the earth trembled. She clenched in fear not making a sound. When she opened her eyes, it took a few seconds for her to make out the long silver reptilian tail above her. As it passed the light returned. She quickly sat up moving her hair out of her face.

She heard a roar. Midair over the horizon flew a dragon, its tail swooshing as it flew. It landed on top of a mountain, spread its veined wings wide, roared again, and disappeared into a mist.

"It's okay Snow, you can come out now," Gwen said, petting his head.

He peeked out, meowed and quickly turned his head into her armpit again. Walking out of the wheat field, she discovered a mulberry tree and stood under its shade as deep purple berries dangled around her. She placed Snow on the ground and started eating the fruit one at a time. The sweet texture brought her pleasure. She knelt down offering one to Snow. He sniffed it and turned his head away.

"Suit yourself," Gwen said as she picked more.

Behind her the sun was setting, turning the sky paradise pink and lilac. Fireflies came out lighting the air with their gleaming glows as Gwen continued eating. Suddenly, the branches and leaves shook as something large flew past. Gwen and all the mulberries fell to the ground. The being that stood behind Gwen lowered its large head. She felt its breath on her neck. She froze for a moment, then slowly turned her head. A large eye was looking right at her, its iris a pool of gold, scarlet, and amethyst. Its pupil long and its eyelid scaly.

The glimmering gold dragon lifted its head and spread its glorious wings in the sunset. Gwen didn't move as it grumbled and lowered its head back to her. Cautiously she reached out her hand toward the dragon. The dragon nodded and stretched its neck, putting its forehead in her palm. She looked at the majestic creature with respect and pet its cheek.

Gathering a handful of berries from the ground, she lifted them to the dragon. Its long slithery tongue licked them up. Gwen grabbed more berries. The juice stained her hands, and she wiped them in the grass. As she did, the dragon left her.

She picked Snow up to go searching for a place to rest in the woods. As the forest darkened, the ground became wet, giving off a whiff of mildew. Weeping willows drooped in sorrow along the way and the ground was covered in a sheet of fog. Her boots became coated with mud. Old tree stumps sported fungus and yellow mushrooms. A green film of algae covered the bog where the decaying vegetation reeked of sulfur and flies buzzed over the murky waters.

"What are you doing in my swamp?" a vicious voice spoke.

Gwen held Snow closer as she looked around but didn't see anything.

"Get out," the malevolent voice warned.

The color drained from Gwen's cheeks. She didn't know which way to go. She kept turning to look in every direction. Small beady red eyes of fire blazed in the bushes, staring as they studied her.

"Please, I don't know where to go," she cried.

The creatures snickered.

"Are you lost?" a defiant voice asked.

"Yes, I am. If you could please just tell me how to get out of here. I won't disturb you again," she pleaded.

"Look boys, we caught ourselves some dinner," the creature's voice carried over the swamp.

The shrubs moved as small slimy green creatures came out of hiding. They surrounded Gwen, their faces covered in snot and boils.

"You hold her down. I'll drain her blood," a goblin wearing a red hood directed.

They wore rags for clothes and had crooked teeth. One laughed profusely and took out a shiny pick. Ready to slaughter her, it grimaced and charged. Gwen jumped, kicking it into the swamp with a splash.

"Get her!" another goblin ordered as the group swarmed.

She hurdled over them carrying Snow as she made a run for it. The goblins with their weapons in hand followed.

"Get her!" they yelled.

Gwen looked over her shoulder. They were gaining on her. She leaped in long strides as her boots spit out dirt, splattering them with mud. The goblins waved their weapons above their heads.

"I'll get her!" a goblin shouted and threw its ax.

The ax spun through the air barely missing Gwen's head and hitting the trunk of a tree. She screamed in terror, ran between two trees and through a spider web covered with dew that clung to her hair. She used one shaking hand to wipe it off.

Another goblin waved its flail releasing it. Gwen jumped, landed in the grass gasping, and looked back. Snow landed on his feet in front of her. She shut her eyes, closing them tight as the weapon hit an invisible barrier. The goblins caught up, but an unseen shield pushed them back knocking them over. A goblin hopped back up on its legs. Angry, he screamed and charged at Gwen. The barrier glistened in gold as the goblin went flying into the pit of the swamp.

"Ah!" it yelled, fading into the distance. "We'll get you next time!"

As Gwen got up covered with mud, leaves and spider webs. She saw the gold dragon standing before her. She ran her fingers through her hair.

"Yuck," she said whacking the crud to the ground.

The dragon opened its mouth releasing a whirlwind that engulfed Gwen. It spiraled around her, and the dragon sucked the air back in leaving her and Snow clean. The dragon bowed and sat. Gwen got on its back and Snow jumped on too. It clawed the earth before taking off into the sky. Gwen held on as they soared through the clouds.

Gwen laughed in disbelief as she looked down. She could see the entire kingdom. Snow purred, looking at her squinting with eyes filled with love and admiration. As she traveled the sky, beyond the mountains she saw a sea with waves crashing to the shore. There was a field of lavender, and a colossal castle made of white and gray stone with a drawbridge and a Victorian garden. The land was filled with forests that spread for miles and miles.

Gwen's hair streamed out behind her as they flew. Gwen held on tight as the dragon looped through the air to a smooth landing. She picked up Snow and slowly climbed off. Then she and Snow curled up with the dragon under an old ash tree. The dragon wrapped its wing over them like a blanket. The stars appeared so close and bright, like twinkling crystals. Gwen imagined grabbing one. The land quieted with the night. With the dragon protecting her and Snow, they slept, soothed with dreams of peace and contentment.

CHAPTER 2
LOST

The snoring of the dragon awoke Gwen. The sun crept from behind the mountain tops saturating the grasslands in a soft yellow light. The tall pale grass was sprinkled with droplets of morning dew. Gwen, wrapped in the dragon's wings, shivered in the cold wind. A blue hare hopped across the fields between the strands of grass, ears brushing through the long wheat. The dragon slowly opened its eyes. Its slit pupils turned towards the morning sun. It yawned revealing a mouth full of fangs and walked out of the shade into the sun, scales glittering in the light.

Gwen and Snow sat by a tree watching their protector. Placing her hand over her mouth, a tired Gwen yawned. She needed to find a place to stay. She walked out into the field under a faded blue sky and inhaled the cold crisp air. She longed for a place away from the wild but had nothing with her except Snow and the clothes on her back.

She wondered what was happening back home, if anyone realized she was missing or was looking for her. She rubbed her eyes thinking perhaps this was all a dream and pinched herself.

"Ow," she yelped, watching the plume made by her breath.

She shivered and rubbed her arms. Bending down she picked up Snow carrying him as she wandered around the woods. The tree trunks and branches, coated with moss every shade of green, stretched over a small creek that flowed over heavy rocks. The rushing waters streamed in eddies around the deep roots of the trees. Distracted by the fascinating sights and sounds, she didn't see the dragon was no longer there.

Why did the book write my name? she thought. *I remember when I was five,* Mom *held it with both hands. The nightlight and a small lamp were on, but the room was still dim.*

The cover of the book was dark. I could not see the title and was never sure if she was reading or making up stories of her own.

"Goodnight my little Princess," she would say and kiss me on the head as she tucked me into bed.

Gwen thought harder and wondered about the pages. They were filled with words but no pictures. She was so little she couldn't read yet. She never saw the book unless her mother had it.

What did it say? Gwen asked herself. *Where did mom even get that book? I wish I had it with me.*

Gwen heard the leaves rustle and turned to look. in that direction. The hare hopped by a bush and hid lowering its ears. When Gwen approached, its ears stood up like antennas. It twitched its whiskers alarmed by the sound and ran deeper into the woods.

There was a vitality to the forest—something that awoke her senses. As she carried on, she heard a sound like the branches brushing against each other. When she turned around, there was nothing. Snow looked up at her giving her a meow.

"Probably nothing," she said.

Gwen thought she saw faces appear in the trunks of the trees with noses, mouths, and eyes of wood. The eyes seemed to follow Gwen's every move. She felt their eyes on her, yet they didn't make a sound. Knowing something strange was happening, she constantly looked over her shoulder.

"We really need to get out of these woods and find a place to stay," she told Snow.

That's when she saw a large antique mirror levitating off the ground. In the mirror was the reflection of the trees and the forest's greenery. Gwen could see herself in it as she got closer. The long oval shaped mirror was almost as tall as she was.

"Why is there a mirror? And why is it just floating there?"

She checked behind it. Everything appeared normal. It had a dark back side just as mirrors do.

The frame was an ornate antique gold. Then something even stranger happened. In the mirror, the tree behind her blinked and took on a menacing deranged look. She turned around to look at the tree. It had a face, but it appeared peaceful. She looked toward the mirror again. The malevolent figure was back. She didn't know if the tree was playing tricks on her or if it was the mirror. She leaned closer and touched the reflection of the tree. As she did, her hand went into the mirror. She peeked her head around to see if her arm extended behind the mirror—it didn't. She pulled her arm out and decided to step through. Snow gave a crying meow as she disappeared.

"That's odd. Must have just been a frame after all," she said. "Come Snow."

When she looked down, she noticed her cat was missing.

"Snow?" She called but didn't see him.

She started walking and things began to change. The sunlight faded to gray until the forest became washed out and grim. The moss and leaves withered. The tree branches became bare, and the ground grew soft and moist.

"Maybe I should go back," Gwen said.

She turned back but the mirror was gone.

"Ah, man," she said with a shrug. "Maybe I'll find it going this way."

Owls hooted in the naked gray trees. Her skin felt clammy, and cold. Every tree trunk focused a vile face on Gwen. Their glares were heavy on her back. Filled with dread, she moved to the center of the road. The trees moaned as if in pain, their branches reaching out toward her. Gwen's heart beat wildly, her breathing grew fast as the branches swooped down. She gasped in fear, leaping away. More branches reached down for her, moaning as they tried to snatch her.

Gwen suddenly realized the sad faces were actually trapped souls. The road before her narrowed. She let out a shrill scream as the ground started to shake. The forest debris fell as the tremors grew stronger. Gwen slipped and fell. Standing back up, she wiped the soil off her dress and started running for her life.

A giant earthworm with a long blue-gray body shot out of the soil. The ginormous worm dove in and out of the ground destroying the road. It roared revealing millions of sharp teeth, and its slimy body left mucus-like goo on the dirt. Gwen screamed and continued running as fast as she could. She looked back at the worm. It was gaining on her. Up ahead, she saw the mirror and sped up. Her chest was heaving, she stood before the mirror and turned around. The worm rose high in the yellow gray sky. Up close, its skin was a fleshy pink and bruised purple. It opened its jaws and gave a loud roar, dripping strings of saliva covering Gwen in its goo. The worm came diving down ready to eat its prey. Gwen fell backwards out of the mirror and landed back in the lush forest.

She quickly rolled over and leaped behind the mirror. She held the frame with both hands as the worm came rushing from the mirror. Gwen turned the mirror's reflection down over the grass. The worm tried to shake her from its back, and her fingers started slipping. She held the mirror as close to her body as she could. The frame vibrated lifting her higher. She closed her eyes riding the turbulence on the worm's back. She and the mirror fell to the ground, shattering it into tiny pieces. She released her hold while remaining on top of the mirror. When the commotion stopped, Snow ran up to her as light shined from every broken piece. Then the mirror disappeared.

"Do you always walk into portals?" a man's voice asked.

"No, actually, I don't. I wasn't sure what that was," Gwen said, breathing heavily as she stood up covered in slime.

"Ew," the man uttered grossed out. "You could use a shower."

"Obviously," Gwen said.

She looked at him but couldn't make out his face through the mucus. She wiped the goop from her eyes and looked up at the man standing before her. He was well kept and no more than a few years older than she was. He was dressed in studded leather armor and boots. He had a baldric that carried a sword strapped over him. His hair was brown above endearing hazel eyes. He was taller than she was, fit and strong.

"So, who are you? And how did you find me?" she asked.

"Oh right. I'm Nicholas and I came because I heard unruly noises. I wasn't sure if an animal was being slaughtered or if someone was in danger.

"I see. Well, I'm okay, thank you. It was kind of you to come and check on me," Gwen said.

"But of course, I wouldn't want you to die out here in these woods."

"Thank you and if I can, I would like to wash up,"

she said.

"I would be happy to help. Say, I've never seen you before. What's your name?" he asked.

"I'm Gwen. I'm not really sure how I got here. My cat ran away, and I went looking for him. Somehow, he led me here and I can't seem to find my way back home. I slept in the fields. Do you know of any place I can stay?" she asked.

"It's nice to meet you, Gwen. Sleeping in the fields is not safe out here in the Dragon Lands. You could have been killed."

"The Dragon Lands?"

"Yes, past these fields are the Dragon Lands. Let me tell you, not all dragons are nice," he explained.

"I'm sorry. I didn't know and I've been lost. I took care of that worm just fine," she said with a grin.

"Perhaps but it's not safe. Get on the back of my steed. I have a place you can stay, and we'll get you cleaned up."

"Okay, but can my cat come too?" she asked.

"Cat? Well, I guess so."

"Thank you so much."

Gwen picked up her kitty as he got on the horse and offered her a helping hand up. She slid her foot into the stirrup as Nicholas took Snow. She put her leg over the horse, took the cat, and wrapped her arms around the strange man with Snow in-between them. Nicholas raised the reins and galloped the black stallion through the forest. The sound of its hooves echoed through the trees. Disturbed, the birds ruffled their feathers and flew up into the blue sky.

The horse neighed when they came out onto a grassy field. Mountains shimmered in the distance, the sun glowing above the peaks. The horse ran up a hill covered with wildflowers.

The golden dragon glided by, passing above them. As if by magic, Gwen was clean and dry again. The dragon waved its tail in the air as it passed. It plummeted past the river rapids and flew down following a long waterfall. The dragon screeched as it lifted itself above the crashing water.

The hill leveled into flatland, and they rode across fields of lavender. Across the way were more woods and a sea. The azure waters spread out with no end in sight. Gwen looked over Nicholas's shoulder and saw a massive castle. As they pushed through the lavender, the steed's long black hair bounced, and its coat shone like smooth silk.

"Heel boy. Heel," Nicholas called, tugging on the reins as it stomped across the drawbridge. The horse whinnied, rearing up on its back legs.

"Whooa, down!"

The animal lowered and trotted to the stables. The stalls were filled with an army of horses. Some neighed while others chewed on the grass. Gwen gave Snow to Nicholas as she got down and adjusted her dress. Nicholas handed her the cat, jumped down, and removed the saddle.

"Wow, what are we doing here?" Gwen asked.

Nicholas turned looking at her, "What do you mean?"

"Why are we at a castle?" she asked.

"Well, you said you needed a place to stay." He paused furrowing his brows.

"Well yeah but a castle? I mean, I wouldn't want to impose. Isn't there an inn somewhere or a tavern?" she asked.

"No, just here. This is the only place unless you want to sleep outside or go back to the forest," he suggested.

"It's just that, I don't know who lives here and I don't want to be a bother," she explained.

"I live here, and you're not a bother," he assured her.

"What? You live here?"

"Of course. After all, I am the Prince," he said dropping the saddle to his side.

"Prince? If you're a Prince, then what are you doing dressed like that?" she asked.

"Dressed like what? I was just going out into the woods. It's nothing formal to get all dressed up for. And around here, you always need to be prepared," he explained.

"Prepared for what?" she asked.

He gave a boyish smile looking at the ground. He looked back up, bit his lip and shook his head. The light hit his hazel eyes reflecting an olive green.

"I already told you. It's dangerous around here. You can never be too careful."

He led the horse to its stall, removed the muzzle stroking him and patted his head.

"Good job today Sheamus," he said as he walked out and locked the wooden door.

"I can take care of myself," she stated.

"Are you sure about that? Because you don't appear to have a weapon, do you?"

"Well, no, but that's only because I got lost. Like I said, I don't know how I got here."

Nicholas shook his head. "It sounds to me like you have a problem. Now, I'm no expert or anything but it's probably best to stay somewhere safe while you get it all figured out. Why don't you come inside?"

"Okay but just so you know, I didn't need you to save me."

"I didn't save you. You saved yourself. I just came to make sure you were okay." He smiled in agreement.

"Thank you, Prince Nicholas."

"You're welcome," he said.

They left the stables and approached the palace doors. The old heavy wooden doors were opened for them by two knights.

"Thank you," Gwen said as she followed the Prince inside.

She stepped into the foyer as the knights slowly closed the doors behind them. She had never seen a grand castle nor been inside one. She rethought her decision to accept the Prince's invitation, but she had nowhere else to go.

Snow ran across the castle to where Gwen stood next to the Prince. Nicholas removed his boots and Gwen did the same. She was mesmerized as she looked around the Victorian palace. She knew it had to be very old. And yet it was so grand and marvelous. The walls were stories high. The ceiling was coffered in copper and burnt umber, its colors warm and comforting. Against the wall was a mango wood credenza. On it was a stained-glass mosaic vase filled with red roses. The floors were tile and covered in paisley maroon runners.

"Nicholas? Is that you?" an old woman's voice called.

Gwen's curiosity quickly dissolved, someone important was approaching. She stood straight and tall as shoes clunked across the palace floor.

"Don't be nervous, meeting the Queen isn't as big of a deal as you think," Nicholas whispered to Gwen and gave her a promising smirk.

Gwen held her hands behind her back with her legs close together. From around the corner stepped an older woman in a red and beige ballgown made of a brocade satin. The woman's hair was faded brown with strands of gray highlights. It was curled in an up-do interwoven with braids. A gold crown decorated with diamonds, pearls, and garnets sat on top of her head. She was covered in gold. She wore a set of onyx earrings held by grape leaves that sat ever so elegantly on her ears. She also had a ring to match with a large marquise stone. It was center wrapped in a gold vine. Her face was dour and wrinkled with wisdom. Dropping the hem of her dress, she folded her hands in front of her and gave Gwen a disapproving look.

"Mother, this is Gwen. I had heard unsettling sounds coming from the woods. She was lost when I found her," Nicholas explained.

The Queen lifted her chin and raised her eyebrows.

"Your Highness." Gwen curtsied.

"Yes well, I see. Welcome to my castle. You're welcome to stay as long as you need," the Queen offered.

"Oh my, that is very kind of you. Thank you." Gwen curtsied again.

"Guards! I want no more visitors and no one else here. You understand?" the Queen demanded.

"Yes, your majesty," an armored man a few feet behind Gwen answered.

"Very good. Griswald!" the Queen called.

A little man came scurrying down the long hall.

"Coming your majesty. I'll be right there," he shouted as he hurried. "Yes, your majesty."

Standing before her, he bowed his head. He had short curly brown hair that ruffled around his small ears, and a handlebar mustache he twirled with his stubby fingers. Under his lip, he had a chin puff. He wore a white button-down shirt, a red bow tie, brown leather belt, suspenders, and polished black shoes. He lifted his head to look at Gwen and Nicholas.

"Griswald..." the Queen paused as she studied Gwen. "This is Gwen. She will be our guest. Please show her to a room and help her get settled in."

"Yes, your majesty."

"I hope my staying here isn't too much trouble," Gwen said.

"So don't make it be," the Queen remarked.

The servant looked at Gwen. "No luggage?" he asked.

"No, I don't have anything," Gwen said.

"Dear, she's probably a drifter." The Queen raised her one eyebrow as she turned and walked away.

Gwen waited until she was out of sight. "She

seems... lovely."

"She is and the Queen is to always be treated with the highest respect. Now, come girl," the servant said.

Gwen looked at Nicholas beside her. He widened his eyes and reached out his arm gesturing for her to follow Griswald.

"Thank you for coming and making sure I was safe. And thank you for letting me stay here. You didn't have to," Gwen said.

"You're welcome. I wasn't going to let you sleep out there and leave you to cuddle with that earthworm tonight."

"Umm... no... That's quite alright," Gwen said and followed the servant down the hall.

The hall was long and narrow but bright at the end. It opened up to all of the castle's glory. The floors were made of marble and the tall windows gave out onto the most breathtaking views of the sea, the mountains, and lavender fields. The furniture was handcrafted Victorian, tufted and upholstered. There were regal burgundy sofas, chairs, and a chaise with graceful curves that matched. The grand walls were framed in crown molding. Table stands and credenzas held candelabras with white tapers. Crystal and gold chandeliers hung down from the ceiling.

Gwen looked up at the dome ceiling with its mural of heaven. It was painted with a blue sky, plump clouds, cherubs, roses, and harps. There was a statue of the Queen against the ivory wall next to the window. Across the room was a statue of a little boy by another window.

"Wow," Gwen muttered under her breath admiring all the beauty.

She then noticed large ivory and gold vases filled with yellow orchids, white hydrangeas, pink peonies, and white roses. Gwen slowly backed up and felt something cold and pointy poke her back. Startled, she turned around to look. It was a statue of a king dressed for battle and holding a sword. He had one knee bent and held his sword in front of him. Gwen looked at the statue puzzled.

"You look familiar. Where have I seen you before?" she said and placed her hand on her chin.

She looked at his eyes when it hit her--this was the ghost she saw.

"Oh my god," she gasped, covered her mouth, and backed away.

"Gwen? Are you coming? Where did you go?" Griswald called.

She turned to her right and ran up the stairs. She reached the second story hallway filled with doors. Another long maroon runner reached all the way to the end of the hall.

"Right this way. Your room," he said as he turned the knob and opened it for her."

"Thank you," Gwen said, stepping inside.

The bedroom walls were faint gold with no luster. To her right was a queen size bed of wood centered against the wall. White and gold blankets with purple and gold throw pillows rested under a matching purple canopy. Near the bed were two glass doors that let out onto a balcony. Across the room standing between the doors and wall was an antique bookcase. Beveled nightstands made of dark wood holding fringe lamps flanked the bed. Natural light illuminated the room.

Gwen liked the room and thought it was sweet. She smiled and dove backwards onto the bed. The comforter fluffed and waved as her head sunk into the feathery pillow. She looked up at the canopy, let out a sigh of comfort and closed her eyes.

"This is the most comfortable bed I have ever been in!" she shouted.

Gwen turned to look out through the glass doors at the clouds drifting by. Laughing, she jumped up heading for the balcony doors, grabbed both handles, and swung them open. A gentle breeze waved through her hair and against her face. She closed her eyes again and continued to smile, taking in a deep breath laced with saltwater air. The sound of seagulls squawking met her ears. She slowly opened her eyes as the wind brushed against her dress. Her hair was soft as it stroked against her cheeks. She looked out at the sea and felt at peace listening to the waves on the sand.

There was a knock at her door, and she headed back inside. Behind her the sky darkened as it transitioned from blue to slate. A gargantuan mass that Gwen didn't see waved long tentacles that broke through the surface. They rose high in the air before splashing down.

"Yes?" Gwen called, opening her bedroom door. "Hello?"

She looked both ways but there was no one in sight. She looked down to see some folded clothes, picked them up, and placed them on the bed. She held up a long sheer pink nightgown with long sleeves and a ribbon tied in a bow. She put the dress back on the bed when she heard a woman scream. Gwen ran out of her room and rushed down the castle stairs to the room with the statues.

"Get that thing away from me!" she heard the woman yell.

Gwen approached two tall white doors and struggled to pull one open. She clenched her jaw putting her back into it when the door finally opened.

"How did that thing get in here?" the woman complained.

Gwen found herself in the dining room. The walls were peridot, and the table seemed miles long. The chairs were cushioned and painted gold. Each seat had silverware wrapped in cloth napkins. Renaissance art decorated the walls as if the palace was telling a story. Tall, lush bouquets of white, green, and yellow flowers sat on the table.

The room was empty.

Gwen hurried around and past the massive table to more doors. Using both hands, she pulled one open and found herself in a hallway as long as the castle itself. It was white with many tall windows, French pink furniture, small, marbled tables, and huge white vases full of hydrangeas, peonies, and roses. Gwen looked down the grand hall lost.

Outside, the sun was going down, hues of pink and purple shined through the windows onto the castle walls. Gwen heard the woman sneeze and turned to her right. The sounds of the people talking grew louder. She followed the sound to the stone kitchen where she saw the Queen.

"Your majesty, it's just a cat. I assure you it won't harm you," Griswald said.

"Get that vile rodent out of here right this instant," the Queen sniffled.

"Snow, come Snow," Gwen called patting her hand on her knee.

Snow gave a scared little meow as he ran up to Gwen. She bent down and he leaped up into her arms. The Queen sneezed again.

"You," she growled.

"I'm so sorry your highness," Gwen said as Snow wrapped his paws around her neck.

The Queen sniffled some more, glaring at Gwen with her inflamed sclera. "You and that foul creature can sleep in the chambers."

"You will do no such thing mother," a stern voice called as Nicholas stepped from behind the Queen. "He can stay with you in your room," Nicholas insisted as he looked at Gwen.

"Dinner will be served in half an hour. Everyone, go get washed up," Griswald instructed.

"Sounds splendid." Nicholas said annoyance curling his lip.

He held his hands behind his back, turned, and

exited through the swinging doors. The Queen looked at Gwen, bothered and annoyed. Gwen held Snow closer to her as he began purring. She walked past the Queen into the dark hall and back into the main room. The castle felt like a maze. To her left were stairs that spiraled down, in front of her was a staircase that spiraled up, and to her right was a door. She walked up the spiraling staircase made of stone with windows that looked out to the mountains.

"I think our room is this way," she said to Snow as her sweet voice echoed.

She was walking up the steps when she heard something scurry in the walls. It sounded like clattering and tapping.

"That's strange. It's probably mice," she muttered.

She walked in what felt like circles when she came across more windows. She finally reached the place that let out to her floor. She found her room and opened the door. Snow ran in, jumped on the bed, and started to purr.

"You wait here okay. I'll bring you some food and water," she said as she slowly closed the door.

She walked out to the main stairs and down to the dining room. This time, the doors were already open. The table was lit with candelabras. There were plates and crystal prism glasses at every seat.

"Please, join us," Nicholas insisted pulling out a chair and offering it to Gwen.

"Thank you. I would love to," she said as she entered the room and took a seat.

The Prince sat across from her.

"Where is everyone?" she asked.

"They're on their way. This room will be full," he said.

"Oh." She gave a shy smile.

A few moments later, a large group of people walked in. The Queen sat all the way at the end of the table. Griswald, guards, knights, a butler, and a woman with long brown hair accompanied by three hobgoblins took their seats.

A knight sat next to Gwen and a hob on her other side. The room quickly filled with chatter as they all celebrated.

"I didn't realize there were so many people living here," Gwen said.

"Oh yes. Well, it is a big castle after all," Nicholas informed her. "Everyone has their own room, and everyone has a duty," he said.

"What does everyone do?" she asked.

"Allow me to introduce you," Nicholas said as he stood, took a fork, and clinked his glass. Everyone, please quiet down. We have someone new joining us I would like you all to meet."

The chatter gradually faded, and all eyes turned on the Prince. Whispers continued until Nicholas cleared his throat and the room went silent.

"Everyone, this is Gwen. I found her lost in the woods. She had nowhere to go that was safe. So, I invited her here. I trust you'll all welcome her and be kind during her stay," he said.

"Why do you think he brought her here?" one guard whispered to a knight.

"Where did she come from?" one hob whispered to another hob.

The hobs' skin was as green as algae. They had long pointy ears on the sides of their heads, wide mouths, pointy little teeth, and yellow eyes. Their noses and faces had boils and warts. They were stumpy little creatures with dirty hands and feet from tending the garden. Their raggedy clothes were soiled, and they had dirt under their sharp nails.

"Ooh, I love fresh meat. I have a few tricks up my sleeve for her," another goblin said with a sinister chuckle.

"Quiet. Now, please help Gwen get settled in. We want her to feel right at home. And no tricks," Nicholas said with a snide glance at the goblins.

They glared at Nicholas, remaining still and mute. After a moment they all chuckled and burst into belly jiggling laughter. One hob lifted its leg and leaned back falling out of his chair. He clunked to the floor and hit his head. He stood back up rubbing it and picked up his chair sitting back in his seat.

"It's nice to meet you all. Thank you for having me," Gwen said as she looked around at everyone.

"Let us feast," Griswald announced as a dozen halflings entered the room walking in through a side door.

Unlike the obnoxious hobs, they were clean and dressed in white shirts and dark brown slacks. They walked with their chins up carrying silver platters. Only three feet tall, they walked erect holding the platters up with their right arms. Folded over their wrists were cloth napkins. Their feet were large, wide and fuzzy with hair. Their ears stuck out from their hair. Gwen wondered if they were servants as they pushed the platters of food onto the table. Gwen felt a tray push against her elbow.

"Thank you," she said as she slid it over in front of herself.

As everyone was presented with food, pitchers of foaming ale were also pushed up onto the table. The halflings took their seats as one man with curly dark brown hair rolled his sleeves up revealing his hairy arms. He had hair sticking out of his ears and nose. He dropped his fists on the table and the ale sloshed.

"Let's eat," he cheered.

Everyone lifted the tops off their platters as a female halfling took out a flute and started playing. She danced and twirled all around the room. Her long auburn hair flowed with her. The room filled with chatter, laughter, and celebration.

The foam coated the hairy halfling's mustache and dripped down his beard. Wiping his face with a hairy arm, he reached across the table for a plate of butter. He ripped his bread apart and slathered butter all over it. Shoving the bread in his mouth, he filled his cheeks in satisfaction. Grease shined on his plump face. He looked over to another halfling and they both laughed. Gwen turned to a halfling standing by her side pouring some ale.

"May I please have some water?" she asked.

The other halflings overheard her question.

"Water?! Hey guys! The new girl wants some water!" a red-headed halfling with a beard and braids said.

Everyone at the table laughed, their bellies jiggling.

"Coming right up," the halfling that poured the ale said.

Gwen stirred her stew while the halfling returned to pour water in Gwen's crystal glass. She ate her stew, dipping her bread in the broth, and sipping water as she watched Nicholas drink his ale.

"Ah, that is some good ale, Harry," Nicholas praised him.

"Here, here!" the hairy halfling shouted.

He pounded his fist on the table, took a pitcher of ale, and chugged it down. The bard stopped playing. The whole room gasped as they watched him. He drank every last drop and then slammed the empty pitcher on the table. Catching his breath, he looked at Nicholas and let out a roaring belch to which the men cheered and applauded.

The bard continued her song, she jumped up on a chair and danced across the table. Her feet stomped, food bounced, and drinks waved. People clapped as she twirled, dipped, and leaped all around. Gwen took a mouthful of stew when she felt something funny in her mouth. She put her finger and thumb in her mouth and pulled out a piece of paper. No one seemed to notice, everyone's attention remained on the bard. Gwen unfolded the paper and read it—Run.

She looked at the Prince who was nodding his head

enjoying the performance. Gwen's eyes widened in fear. She quickly got up from the table and ran out of the room, up the stairs and down the hall. Making her way to the bedroom, she grabbed Snow and quickly searched the room. Hurrying back down the stairs, she looked both ways and made her way down the dark hall to the foyer holding Snow close. She found the way blocked by two guards.

"Excuse me but, I must leave now," she said in a panic.

"What is the meaning of this?" Nicholas appeared behind her.

"I'm sorry, I have to go. I can't stay."

"What's wrong?" he asked.

"Nothing, I just have to go."

"Well, calm down. It's dark outside. It's night and hard to see out there. You'll get lost. Something could happen to you. There are a lot of creatures lurking in the dark. Why don't you rest. If you really want to leave, you can in the morning. We won't make you stay if you don't want to."

Gwen, no longer afraid, calmed down. "Why do you care what happens to me?"

"Well I... I care about everyone here in the castle. I don't want to see anyone hurt, that's all. You're our guest. We want to make sure you're safe. You're free to leave whenever you'd like. But I strongly suggest you do so when it's daylight."

"Why are you so kind to me?" her voice softened.

"Well, I'm the Prince. It is my duty to ensure the safety and preservation of the land and all its beings. It is my obligation to watch out for all living things in the kingdom. Please, wait until daylight. If you must leave, I can have someone take you where you want to go. At least then I'll know you'll get there safely," he said.

"I don't understand." Gwen choked up and began to cry.

"What's wrong? What is it?"

"It's just that I don't know where I am. I want to go home but, I don't know how to find my way back. I don't know if I'm safe here. There was a piece of paper in my dinner that told me to run."

"Hey, it's alright. You're safe here. No one is going to hurt you. No one wishes you any harm," he assured her as he lowered his head and met Gwen's tear-filled eyes. "Look at me. You see these guards? The knights? They'll keep you safe. They ensure all of us are safe at all times. If there's a threat, they'll handle it. Okay?"

"Okay," she said as she sniffled and nodded her head.

Nicholas wrapped his arms around her neck and embraced her. Her head met his chest as she closed her eyes and wiped away her tears.

He released his hold and slowly drew back. "Come finish your dinner. You must be hungry from wandering for so long," he said.

"I am."

"Come on, it's okay. Someone was just trying to scare you. They thought it was funny pulling a prank. I bet it was one of the hobs," he said as they walked back to the dining room.

When they returned, everyone was gone, and the room had been cleared. All that remained was their food.

"Thank you," she said.

The Prince sat back down in his chair. "You're welcome. If there's anything you need or anything we can do to make you feel better or more comfortable– just let someone know. I will see that it gets taken care of," he promised.

Gwen looked at the Prince and smiled. "I wonder why someone would put that note in my stew?"

"I don't know. Those hobs are mischievous little creatures. They love playing tricks and pranks," he said.

"Well, I certainly didn't find it funny." she said.

"Neither do I. I'm glad you feel better now," he said sipping his ale.

"I do, thank you for well—everything—all of this. I never expected any of it and you didn't have to help me," she said.

"You're welcome. You wouldn't want to be out there all alone in the rain and cold. The least I could offer you was a room and some food," he said.

"And the food is delicious. I can't remember the last time I ate something this good," she said.

"All the fruit and vegetables are freshly picked. Madeleine and the hobs tend the garden. They plant, grow, and care for everything. You should see it sometime," the Prince offered.

"Madeleine? Was she at dinner?" Gwen asked.

"Yes, she is the lady of the garden as we call her. She has long brown hair," he said.

"Oh, right. I know who she is now. I can't wait to get to know everyone better." Gwen smiled.

"Get to know everyone? Does that mean you've changed your mind and are going to stay?" he asked.

"I think so. I don't feel scared anymore and you reassured me."

"Well, I'm glad. Are you still hungry? Would you like some water?" he asked.

"No, that's okay. Thank you for dinner. I had a wonderful time. I think I'll go to bed," she said.

"Okay, well if there's anything you need, you can let Griswald or one of the guards know. We do have a butler. His name is Gerald. He also keeps a close eye on things," Nicholas explained.

"I do need some food, water, and a litter box for Snow. Also, I don't know where any of the bathrooms are," she said.

"Very well. I will ensure food and water is brought to your room for Snow. I will also have a litter box made for him and will have someone show you where the bathrooms are.

There are thirty-six bedrooms and fifty-one bathrooms.

"Wow, that's a lot of rooms and bathrooms,"

"It takes more than you think to run a kingdom,"

"You're right. I have no idea what it entails, you're a busy man Nicholas."

"I am and that's alright. You must be tired."

"Yes, I haven't slept very well in a few days,"

"I can't imagine anyone sleeping well out in the wilderness. Sleep well. I hope to see you in the morning," he said.

"You too. Thanks again for dinner," she said pushing her chair under the table.

She went upstairs, Snow following at her side. When they reached the hall to her room, he walked in front of her waving his tail.

"Miss Gwen," a voice called.

She turned to see Griswald and a tall guard approaching. He spoke as Gwen turned the knob, opening the room.

"We brought some food bowls, dinner, water, and a litter box for Snow upon your request."

"Yes, thank you very much," she said as they placed the items on the floor.

"Very well. Also, across the hall on the right is a full bath. A few more doors down is a powder room. Both have towels, soap, and other amenities. Please let us know if there's anything else you need."

"I think I'm good for tonight but thank you. I will be heading to bed. Thank you for bringing the stuff for Snow." She smiled as the cat curled up in the middle of the bed.

"No problem at all. Make sure he doesn't get out and disturb the Queen again. She doesn't like cats—or many creatures really." Griswald rolled his eyes.

"I will do my best. Goodnight," Gwen said.

"Goodnight," Griswald said as Gwen closed the

door.

Gwen lifted her dress over her head revealing her curves. Her skin was soft, and sun kissed. Sliding a pink nightgown over her bare shoulders, she stretched allowing the gown to slide down her body. She lifted her hair out from under the fabric. She placed Snow's food, water and litterbox in the corner of the room.

Exhausted, she cozied in bed and laid her head on the plush pillow. Pulling the gold threaded comforter over her, she closed her eyes. They flew back open when the room shook. Startled, Gwen looked out the balcony doors as the gold dragon flew past, its scales shimmering in the moonlight. It returned flying slowly, its slit eyes looking at Gwen. She hopped out of bed and opened the balcony doors.

"Were you looking for me?" she whispered.

The dragon exhaled, its red and purple eyes blinked as it watched her. She stepped closer to the rail, got on her tip toes and reached out her hand. The dragon bowed its head and closed its eyes. Gwen placed her hand on its snout.

"What is your name?" she asked.

The dragon slowly lifted its head, fixing its gaze on Gwen.

"Leux," it grumbled in an old man's voice.

"Leux," She mumbled under her breath.

She drew her hand back dropping it to her side as the wind picked up and the dragon turned to fly into the night sky glistening in the moonlight, its form reflected in the calm waters. Gwen twirled in excitement as it waved its tail.

The dragon vanished and Gwen stepped back inside. She closed the doors against the wind, got back in bed, and pulled the covers up. Snow curled up on the pillow next to her. Pulling the covers over her head, Gwen buried her face in the pillow and drifted off to sleep.

CHAPTER 3
MIDNIGHT MOON

The bright sun shined through the balcony windows and the birds whistled their song. Snow kneaded her hair, lifted his head and yawned. He looked toward the doors curious about the birds. Stretching himself, the cat jumped down and slowly walked to the door fluffy tail waving in the air. Sitting on the balcony rail was a tree swallow. Snow stood on his back legs leaning on the glass door as he watched the bird. He waved his paw and pressed on the door. Gwen let out a sleepy sigh and slowly opened her eyes. She squinted as her eyes adjusted to the light.

"How am I still here?" She wondered aloud.

Gwen thought it was all a dream and expected to awaken in her own bed. She sat up and stretched, looking over at Snow who was still admiring the bird. Her bare feet delicately met the floor as she stood and walked over to the door. She knelt down picking up Snow in her arms.

"Good morning baby," she said giving him a kiss on his cheek.

His eyes remained fixed on the chirping swallow. It twitched its little blue head, spread its wings, and flew away as Gwen opened the door and stepped out. The sun shined on Gwen's blonde hair as she watched the waves. Breathing deeply, she looked up at the sky. It was the bluest sky she had ever seen with ginormous plump clouds. Gwen felt as if she could reach out and touch them. Serenity washed over her as she listened to her own breathing soft and low. She closed her eyes inhaling as she took it all in. Gwen felt free.

Snow wrapped his paws around her neck holding her tighter. Gwen gave him a hug as she turned around and closed the doors behind her. She placed Snow on the bed and sat down beside him as he continued to purr. Her mind wandered to her past, to her career and people always complaining to her. How they yelled and blamed her for every small problem. She thought about the feces in the fitting rooms, being yelled at over dirty change, and having customers throw piles of clothes at her. She thought about Daniel and how he betrayed her.

A knock on her door returned her to the present.

"Just a minute," she said as she wiped her face and went to answer the door.

"Good morning Ms. Gwen. Glad to see you're up early. Please get washed up and changed. The Queen has requested you join her for brunch. Here are some clothes," Griswald said handing them to Gwen.

"The Queen?" Gwen questioned taking the clothes.

"Yes, I know. I thought the same thing. Well anyway, she's requested you meet her in the garden. Do hurry," Griswald instructed as he turned and walked away.

Gwen watched him walk down the hall before closing her bedroom door to change. She placed the clothes on her bed and sat back down.

Maybe being here isn't so bad after all, Gwen thought. *Maybe I shouldn't go back. I can start over here. Maybe I can live a better life and be happier.*

Gwen sighed and looked at the clothes beside her, admiring the purple and gold.

"What does she want me to wear?" Gwen asked.

She stood up unveiling an intricate Victorian ballgown of royal purple with gold accents. The embroidered dress had long flared sleeves with sparkles. The matching hat was slightly tilted with gold feathers and purple roses in different shades.

"Wow. Well, this is.... uh... extra," Gwen said admiring the gown.

She searched the dresser where she found a golden hairbrush. She brushed her hair, and in another drawer discovered a bottle of perfume. She sprayed it in the air in front of her and sniffed.

"Ugh," she uttered in dislike.

She placed the perfume back in the drawer before putting on the dress and hat. On the bed sat a pair of gold satin gloves that had been hidden underneath the gown. Gwen slipped them on as she left her room and headed down the stairs. She lifted the dress and carried it a few steps when she noticed Nicholas standing below. His eyes grew wide, he raised his eyebrows and smiled.

"Gwen, there you are," he greeted her.

She reached the bottom of the stairs, and the Prince offered his hand.

"Good morning," she said.

"Good morning, Gwen. You look exquisite."

His eyes on hers, he kissed her hand. He was dressed in royal attire, red pants with a gold stripe down the sides, white jacket with gold buttons, a red collar, and red belt. Gwen was drawn into Nicholas's eyes and adorable smile.

"Would you please show me to the garden?" she asked.

"Yes of course."

Together they walked the grand hall to a glass door.

"Right this way," Nicholas grinned and held the door for her.

The castle's greenhouse was the most magical place Gwen had ever seen. It was a giant dome of glass with gold plates and bars, five stories high.

Finches, hummingbirds, bluebirds, and yellow canaries sang as they flew freely. There were bird houses and feeders all around. The greenhouse was filled with ferns, geraniums, petunias, pansies, succulents, eucalyptus, anemone, and bright eyes.

This was also where the hobs grew the food. They tended to the plants, spraying them with water, and keeping a watchful eye on them. Madeleine supervised the hobs and checked the health of the tomatoes, mushrooms, rosemary, thyme, berries, and more grown there.

"Hello Gwen," Madeleine called from a distance.

As she came closer, Gwen could see that her gloves and overalls were covered in dirt, and she had dirt on her face. Her hair was in two braids.

"Hello Madeleine, you sure do start early," Gwen commented.

"We usually start at five or six in the morning. That's when the plants greet the sun. Taking care of the food requires great care and attention to detail. I see you're dressed for brunch."

Sweat beaded on her forehead and Madeleine wiped her brow with her arm.

"It is hot in here. You should have some water," Gwen suggested.

"I'll be fine. We have to keep the greenhouse at a specific temperature. Have you had a chance to take a look around?" she asked.

"Oh yes. It's beautiful here." Gwen smiled.

"Have you seen the pond?"

"No, where is it?"

"Follow me," Madeleine replied.

They walked by carrots and potatoes as they approached the small pond. Lily pads and bright purple lotuses floated at the surface. Gwen noticed perch, catfish, and salmon in the pond that was flanked by pomegranate and orange trees. To the left was a wooden bridge.

"This place is amazing. Maybe I can help out some time," Gwen offered.

Madeleine crossed her arms and asked, "Have you ever farmed or kept a garden before?"

"Well, no, but you can teach me," Gwen suggested.

The gardener lowered her head shaking it and smirked. "That's alright. It was kind of you to offer. The hobs and I have it under control. You better go meet the Queen. She doesn't invite just anyone to brunch," she said turning back to check the lettuce.

"This place is amazing," Gwen whispered to the Prince.

"I'm glad you like it. The castle is full of surprises," he said.

Nicholas led Gwen over the bridge so she could see all of the greenhouse. On the other side of the pond stood a tall oak tree reaching nearly to the glass ceiling. Alongside it were peach trees, pear trees, and apple trees. They approached another glass door, and Gwen could see lemon trees, rose bushes, and peonies. Nicholas opened the door and together they walked into the garden where a cobblestone path was laid out before them.

The garden was decorated in greenery and Victorian sculptures of cherubs among the daisies, daffodils, and gardenias. Birds flew overhead and dipped in their baths next to pink English roses as they strolled along the path. Near some cherry trees they came upon a large statue of a dragon made of stone. It was taller than Gwen and stood on a rock holding a crystal orb in its claw. She admired the figure and the texture of its scales.

White and yellow butterflies fluttered around them when he reached the side of the castle where roses climbed up the stone. In the center of the garden was a towering granite fountain surrounded by white, yellow, and pink petunias. Across the way from its serene flowing water, the Queen sat at a white table. She was dressed like Gwen except she wore white and pink. She had lace gloves and a pink hat with peonies.

"Well then, I'll leave you to it," Nicholas said.

He left her near where Queen Helena sat elegantly sipping a cup of tea. The Queen didn't seem to notice until Gwen got closer.

"Ah, there you are Gwen. Please, won't you join me?" She put her cup down on a small plate.

"Your majesty." Gwen curtsied and sat down in a chair across from Helena.

"I asked you here so we could talk. I'd like to get to know you better. After all, you just arrived and I know nothing about you," the Queen said, looking up at Gwen from under her hat.

"Yes, of course. Thank you for inviting me," Gwen replied.

"Tell me about yourself, Gwen. Where are you from?" she asked.

"I'm from a small town called Crystal Meadows. Have you heard of it?" Gwen asked.

"No but that's alright. Go on," the Queen insisted, sipping her tea.

"Well, I work in a clothing store. I have a small home. I had a husband, but he left me for another woman," Gwen explained.

"A husband? And he committed adultery? Is that what you're telling me?" the Queen exclaimed, the cup rattling in her hand.

"Well, uh... yes. I met her one night in town and she had his photo," Gwen continued.

"Young lady, any man who is disloyal and commits adultery is no man at all. You're better off without him. You don't need him in your life. He's a common philanderer," the Queen squawked.

"Yes, I agree. That's why I'm not quite sure if I want to return home. Perhaps I'll find somewhere to start anew," Gwen said.

"I can assure you that you're here because my son has taken a liking to you. It's not often he brings a lady around."

"Oh, I see. Well, he has been very kind to me," Gwen said.

"As he should be. You're welcome to stay here in *Sir Jericho's Kingdom* as long as you'd like," the Queen offered.

"Thank you, that is awfully kind. Is that the name of this place? Is there a town anywhere or an inn? I don't want to overstay my welcome here," Gwen told her.

"Nonsense. It's no problem at all, the castle is plenty big enough," the Queen said.

"If I may ask, who is *Sir Jericho*?" Gwen questioned.

"He was the King and my husband. He died in the war," the Queen said.

"Oh... I'm so sorry."

"Don't be. He fought for this land and its people. My husband is a hero," the Queen explained.

"Was that a statue I saw of him inside the castle?" Gwen asked.

"Yes, it is. There are sculptures of the King, me, and Nicholas as a boy," the Queen explained.

"It's interesting. I think I may have seen him before," Gwen said, tilting her head.

"Oh, I'm sure you have. He was the King after all," the Queen replied not seeming to understand Gwen's comment.

Gwen looked at the Queen and realized she was not very old and full of wisdom and stories. During their conversation, a hob dressed as a waiter came from behind a corner carrying two silver platters. He placed one before the Queen and the second in front of Gwen.

"Thank you." Gwen smiled.

The hob didn't speak as he looked at Gwen with

annoyance.

"Francis do bring us the pear champagne," the Queen ordered.

"Right away madame." The hob lifted the lids from the food. "Roasted duck with a pomegranate glaze, Your Majesty."

"This looks wonderful. Thank you so much," Gwen exclaimed.

"Champagne coming right up," he said as he walked back around the corner.

"The castle is magnificent. The greenhouse and garden are so beautiful," Gwen complimented the Queen.

"Yes, we have a chicken coop as well. We have everything we need here," the Queen explained.

"That's amazing. I'm sure there are still a lot of people I have yet to meet," Gwen said.

The hob was back at the table with two glasses. "The champagne," he said.

Using his sharp claw, he twisted the cork until it popped and poured the gold fizzling liquid.

"Anything else your highness?" he asked.

"No, that is all for me. Gwen is there anything else you'd like?" she asked.

"Well, do you by chance have any..." Gwen's question trailed away when the hob blatantly ignored her and walked off.

"Oh, never mind," Gwen uttered under her breath.

"Goblins don't have the best manners," the Queen said, taking a sip of champagne.

After brunch, Gwen headed back upstairs to her room to change. She found herself curiously fascinated by the castle and all the rooms she hadn't seen. In her own room, she noticed a bookcase filled with poetry, tales, and lore. Her eyes flew over the titles, *A Flower's Wish*, *The Clock Tower*, *The Gold Sword*, *A Midnight's Kiss*, *Penelope's Dream*, and then—*Gwen*.

Her eyes quickly ran back over the books. *Gwen*

was gone. All she found was a plain green book with no title. She stared at the book momentarily dazed.

"You!" she exclaimed. "I know it's you. You can't fool me."

Gwen pulled the book from the shelf, closely looking at the plain green cover. As she held it, the book began slowly disappearing before her eyes until it vanished into nothing.

"What?" Gwen uttered, frustrated and confused. "Okay, maybe this is all a dream. Maybe I'm in a deep sleep or have been sleeping for too long."

"Did I fall into a coma? Oh my god what if I'm in a coma."

Suddenly, the bookcase started rocking, revealing a hidden door. Gwen stepped forward to take a look. A concrete staircase led down into the dark. There were also stairs leading up. She headed down the staircase where torches mounted on the stone walls lit the way. Distant moans and whimpers echoed along the long flight of stairs. Pausing, she took a moment to look back up before continuing down. The temperature dropped and Gwen began to shiver, and the dreadful sounds grew louder.

"I don't want to hear your whining. Eat your bread," a cruel voice said.

Being quiet as a mouse, Gwen slowed. Chains and shackles rattled nearby. Reaching the bottom of the steps, she hid behind a wall.

"Look at you. You're all a bunch of ungrateful whiners," the same voice bellowed.

Gwen peeked from behind the wall to see the glum, sullen faces of people locked in cells. Hobs slid trays of food to them. The frail, scrawny men appeared malnourished, and the cells reeked of sewage and body odor. The small windows let in only the tiniest amount of light.

"Now I don't want to hear anymore complaining

from you thieves and fornicators," another hob
growled.

Gwen's foot slipped. The goblin quickly turned
looking in Gwen's direction. She made a run for it
back up the staircase. When the room was quiet,
Gwen made her way back down, taking a lighted torch
from the wall. On the dungeon floor, a man, no more
than skin and bones, with a long gray beard was
crying. She gasped seeing the dirty prisoners and the
rags they wore.

As she walked past a cell, chains sounded on the
ground. A man with missing teeth and dull knotted
hair ran up to the front of his cell and grabbed the
bars.

"Please, please, help me! Get me out of here! I'll do
anything! Anything you want!" he cried in desperation.

"I'm... I'm sorry... I can't help you..." Gwen said
nervously as she walked away.

"Please! Help us! Open the cell!" more voices cried
to her.

She kept going when there came the sound of a
door opening.

"The hobs," she uttered under her breath.

She ran the length of the dungeon, finally reaching
a hall that opened in both directions. Not knowing
which way to go, she decided to turn right. As the
sounds grew further and further away, she calmed
down. She reached a large, heavy wooden door with a
circular pattern on it and placed the torch on the
ground. Fearing the hobs would catch her, she slowly
opened the door. Thankfully, it didn't make a sound.
She went inside, closing it behind her. The room was
warmer, and Gwen sighed with relief.

She took a few steps and heard heavy, rumbling
breathing. Laying on the ground before her was a
black dragon. Its eyes were closed in sleep, its nostrils
flaring as it breathed. The room was enormous but
dimly lit. Gwen didn't make any sudden moves. She

sat on the ground and looked up at the dragon with its shimmering scales and its long tail. As the dragon slept, white smoke blew from its nose.

The stone walls were dusty and bleak. On one side of the room was a mountain of bones. On the other side, more bones were scattered about. None of the skulls appeared to be human. Realizing that she was locked in a room with a horned shadow dragon, she began to fidget. Placing her hand on the ground beside her, she felt something wet and slick—blood. She covered her mouth so she wouldn't scream.

She got up and headed back towards the door. As her hand touched the knob, the dragon became silent. Gwen slowly turned to look. The dragon's violet eyes were open. As the dragon arose from its slumber, Gwen's bloody hands trembled on the doorknob. The dragon's nostrils flared. It opened its fang-lined mouth and roared. Gwen quickly opened the door, stepped through, pulled it closed behind her, and ran as fast as she could through the dungeon.

"She woke the dragon!" a prisoner cried.

"What did you do that for?" another prisoner at the steel bars asked.

Gwen ran around a corner and up another flight of stairs, where she reached another door. Exiting, she closed it behind her and found herself outside the castle in between the stables and the garden. Beyond her lay the sea, above her was her bedroom balcony. The sun was setting over the waters and the wind was picking up. Looking up, she noticed there were gargoyles blended into the castle's stone.

"Where did those come from? They weren't there before. I could have sworn those were not there," Gwen said to herself. "Maybe I just didn't notice them before."

The sounds of footsteps were approaching. Checking to see that the coast was clear, she hurried over to the stables.

"Gwen, there you are. What are you doing out here?" Nicholas asked as he approached her.

"Oh, I was just checking on Sheamus and wanted to say hi," she said.

"Oh, I see. You know, I think he likes you."

"You do?" she asked.

"Oh yes, he isn't always this friendly with everyone. He did let you ride him. Did you offer him your hand?" he asked.

"No, I don't want him to be scared of me."

"Nonsense. Come here, I'll show you," the Prince insisted.

He opened Sheamus's stall and brought him out. His coat shined under the peach and lilac filled sky.

"Go ahead, slowly offer him your hand," Nicholas suggested.

Gwen looked at the Prince and back at the steed. She slowly reached out her hand. The horse came closer, bowed his head putting his muzzle in her palm.

"Look at that, he trusts you." Nicholas smiled.

"Yeah, I guess so. Hello Sheamus."

"Would you like to try brushing him?" the Prince asked.

"That would be great,"

Her starry eyes met his as Nicholas went to grab a brush. Gwen stayed with Sheamus, continuing to slowly stroke his muzzle.

"Here, let me show you how," he said, holding the brush in his right hand and slowly stroking the horse's coat. Stand right here."

Nicholas placed Gwen in front of him and reached around her waist, guiding her hand with his and worked the brush.

"Just like that. Go ahead, give it a try," he insisted.

"Okay." Gwen grinned and followed in the same motion as she brushed Sheamus.

"See, you're great at this. Maybe you can ride him

again sometime," Nicholas offered.

"I would like that." Gwen looked into the Prince's eyes and smiled.

"Well, we better head in and get washed up for supper," he said.

"Goodnight Sheamus," Gwen said looking back at the horse.

Nicholas took the horse back to its stall. The sun was setting and at the castle gate were another two gargoyles. Gwen was still unsure whether she missed them or if they had been there before. They walked back inside the castle where Nicholas was greeted by Griswald.

"Your majesty, it is my duty to inform you of tonight's full moon," the halfling said.

"Is that so? Is that tonight already?" the Prince asked.

"Yes, your Highness. We have everything ready," Griswald assured him.

"Very good. Then, I must turn in early for the evening. And Griswald..."

"Yes, your Majesty?" he asked.

"Please, ensure our guest's safety," Nicholas said looking Griswald in the eye.

"Of course, your Majesty. Everything is in order and under control," Griswald reassured him once more.

Gwen, a few feet away behind the Prince, thought nothing of their conversation. Her eyes were studying the castle when a gray figure flew past. A gargoyle landed and quickly blended into the castle. What appeared alive for a moment quickly became stone. Gwen remained fixed on the image when the Queen's shoes tapped across the marble, approaching the Prince in what seemed a panic.

"Nicholas, I must speak with you at once," the Queen demanded.

"What is it mother?"

"The gargoyles, they're back. They've taken their places around the palace."

Gwen turned to see the Queen's face was flushed.

"What's wrong with gargoyles?" Gwen innocently asked.

"Well, there's nothing wrong with gargoyles," Nicholas said.

"My dear, the gargoyles only appear when they need to protect something. They come to warn us of impending danger. Guards! Secure the perimeters!" the Queen ordered.

"Danger? What danger?" Gwen grew worrisome.

"We don't know. All we know is that we must take every precaution possible. The moon is full *tonight*, Nicholas," the Queen stressed to him.

"Yes, I know. Everything is in order and under control."

"What's wrong with a full moon? It's just the moon," Gwen said.

The Queen gave Gwen a surprised look and ignored her remark.

"I'll have the hobs bring supper up to your rooms," the Queen told Nicholas.

"Very well. I better get going. Gwen, lovely to see you. Everyone stay safe and have a good night."

"We all better get to bed early. Who knows what's coming. We will need our rest. Don't worry, the guards will keep watch through the night," the Queen told Gwen.

Everyone retreated to their rooms. The hobs delivered supper to her door on platters. When done eating, she left the platters in the hall. Gwen found it rather peculiar that the castle was quiet so early. She stayed in her room with Snow and waited until everyone was asleep. Outside the full moon was rising. That high up in the castle, it appeared three times its size. Its blue glow illuminated the clouds and reflected on the water. Gwen opened the doors and went to stand on the balcony. It was peaceful and quiet, nothing seemed out of the ordinary. Leaning over the ledge, she looked at a gargoyle that appeared like any other statue.

"I know you're alive. I saw one of you fly around the castle," she said.

When she spoke, the gargoyle's eyes lit up a bright blue. It didn't move or speak but grumbled.

"What danger is coming?" she asked.

Her question went unanswered as the eyes faded back into stone. She looked out to the sea where the surface glittered under the moon. As the winds picked up, so did the sounds of the water. Clouds floated by uncovering glimmering stars, each one like a diamond. Silhouetted against the mountains, Leux flapped his golden wings, and he soared across the kingdom.

"Leux." Gwen leaped in excitement. "Leux!"

But he flew behind the mountains and disappeared into the Dragon Lands. Still, she felt comforted knowing Leux was close by. She went back inside and closed the balcony doors before slowly opening her bedroom door. Sticking her head into the hall, she looked both ways. All was quiet. Not far away, she heard snoring. Snow jumped down from the bed and he rubbed himself against Gwen's legs.

"You stay here," Gwen whispered.

She snuck down the hall, lurking at every door and corner, as she headed for the stairs and the main floor. Wondering if the castle had any other hidden doors, she searched the sculptures of the royal family for any hidden buttons. She pulled on the statues' hands. Still nothing. She walked over to the statue of the king. Looking at him spooked her.

"Why did you come to me?" She wondered aloud.

She pressed around on him, but nothing happened. Then, she heard something scurry. The sound drew her to the kitchen. Deciding it was nothing, she returned to her search. She gently pulled on the king's hands. Again, nothing happened. A loud crash in the kitchen startled her. She tiptoed, following the noise and slowly pushed the door open to take a peek. A pan was still wobbling on the floor from its fall. She didn't notice anything else amiss. Entering the kitchen, she was greeted by the sweet aroma of nectarine tea and deeply breathed in the succulent scent.

Going to the cupboard, she grabbed a teacup and poured some. There was a container of honey dripping on the counter. She took a spoonful and added it to the tea. As she stood there stirring, a cabinet door opened and quickly slammed shut.

Gwen gasped alarmed and placed her cup on the counter. A cabinet door opened and from the shadows appeared a little creature. It stood only about a foot tall with a round belly and short curly brown hair. He wore ripped brown pants and a small dirty shirt that resembled a dish rag.

"What are you doing?' the creature asked infuriated. "Are you stealing our honey?"

"Stealing? No," Gwen assured the little creature.

"That's our honey. You give it back right now." The creature clenched its fists and stepped forward.

"I was only having a cup of tea. I'm so sorry. Please, forgive me. Here, for you," Gwen insisted, sliding the cup over.

The little being's face returned to its normal color, and it relaxed its hands.

"Who are you?" the creature asked.

"I'm Gwen. I just arrived and have only been here a couple of days. Again, I do apologize," she said.

"Don't do it again," the creature warned.

Just then another cabinet slowly popped open and yet another creature came out. It climbed down the cabinets onto the counter.

"She doesn't look threatening. I think she's okay,"

it said as a third creature came out from behind the first.

"What are you?" Gwen wondered.

"We're brownies of course. We clean and take care of the castle," a girl said.

"How come I haven't seen you before?" Gwen asked.

"Well we don't really like humans, nor do we trust you. You're all lazy," the girl stated as she crossed her arms in annoyance.

"Lazy? Well, that's not true about all humans." Gwen said.

"Oh, is it now? Then why do we and the hobs have to do all the housework? Did you hear that, Harold? Maybe we should leave. We're not needed anymore."

"Leave? Don't be silly. I'm just saying not all of us humans are the same. That's all. So, you like honey?" Gwen asked.

"Oh yes. We love honey. It's our favorite food," a boy brownie said.

"I see. Have you ever tried mango honey?" Gwen asked.

"Mango honey? Who would want to ruin perfectly good honey? Honey is perfect just the way it is," the boy stated.

"I'm just saying there are many different varieties and flavors. There's also cream and milk. Have you ever tried warm milk with honey?" Gwen asked.

"Why are you messing with us? What do you want?" the girl asked.

"I don't want anything. Perhaps I'll bring you some mango honey, milk, or cream for you to try some time," Gwen said.

"Why are you being so nice to us? And shouldn't you be in bed? You don't want to be awake at midnight," the girl warned.

"Why? What happens at midnight?" Gwen asked.

"You don't want to know. You don't need to know.

Off to bed and make it fast," a brownie ordered, pushing Gwen's arm with all of her strength but only managed to nudge her.

"I don't understand. Why is everyone around here acting so strange?" Gwen asked.

"She doesn't know," one brownie whispered.

"She doesn't need to know!" the girl shrieked.

"Know what? What is everyone hiding from me?"

"Please Miss, it really is best for you to go back to your room and go to bed," the boy brownie insisted.

"I don't think so. I think I'll stay up and wait to see what happens at midnight," Gwen said.

"That isn't a good idea. It's dangerous for you to be out here. Return to your room at once," the girl demanded. "There are only a few minutes to midnight. Please, let me walk you back to your room. You're tired and not thinking straight."

"Oh okay. I suppose I'll go back to my room," Gwen agreed.

"Lovely, thank you for coming miss. Please, don't steal our honey again." The girl pushed Gwen's arm again.

"I won't, I swear it. And I will bring you some cream or honey another time. Have a nice night," Gwen said.

She left the kitchen and went back to her room. But the suspense kept Gwen intrigued. She sat on her bed while outside, thunder cracked in the clouds. Gwen walked over to the bookcase. The green book was gone. She pressed down on the shelf where it once sat, and the bookcase opened up onto a staircase. She stepped inside and headed up the spiraling stairs where torches lit the way. At the end, there was a hallway. She stepped out as thunder roared again and the rain came down harder.

The long hallway looked as if it led all the way to the other side of the castle. She followed it as lightning flashed outside. She made it halfway across when the floor creaked. Gwen quickly drew her foot back and looked around to see if anyone saw her. But there was no one in sight. On one wall hung a portrait of the royal family. To her right, she saw a bedroom. The door was closed but through it she heard the Queen snoring. She snuck past a few doors when she heard the sound of chains.

"Do they have more prisoners up here?" Gwen whispered to herself.

At the other end of the hall stood an old antique grandfather clock. She looked at the clock as it ticked.

Just thirty seconds until midnight.

Gwen walked closer to another room that gave off unusual sounds. The noises grew louder. It was the chains again. That's when she heard what sounded like a man sigh. She got down on her knees, placed her hands on the wood, and peeped through the keyhole. The moonlight shed through a window silhouetted the figure of a man. He sat on the floor with his legs spread out in front of him, face hidden in the shadows. He sniffled as he were crying.

"Nicholas?" Gwen called.

The Prince looked at the door, his sad face clear in the moonlight.

"Oh my god, Nicholas. Hold on, I'll get you out of there." Panicked, she quickly stood up.

"No. Please, go away. You have to leave. Now!" the Prince warned.

She tried the doorknob, but it was locked.

"Nicholas!" Gwen cried, pounding on the door with her fist. "Hold on!"

Gwen heard a big ferocious roar that shook the floorboards beneath her. She looked through the keyhole again. The Prince's mouth was opened wide to show large teeth. His eyes merged together into one as he grew taller and taller. He ripped off his clothes. Barbaric and savage looking, he released another beastly roar. Gwen helplessly slid her hand down the door and sat on the floor paralyzed in fear.

The Prince had become a cyclops. He rocked the cage with his big hairy hands, breaking the chains that held him. Gwen couldn't believe her eyes. She got up off the floor and ran down the hall and hurried down the stairs as the Prince groaned and roared again.

Back in her room, she quickly closed the bookcase. Gwen got on her bed and curled into a ball. Not only did Nicholas sound monstrous, but he also sounded as if he was in pain. The rain turned into a downpour; lightning flashed outside the balcony doors while she cried burying her head in a pillow. Distraught and shocked, she took a moment to breathe.

"Snow, we're getting out of here. We're leaving first thing in the morning," she cried as the kitty laid in front of her.

She pulled him close as he comforted her. The image of the crazed beast was burned in her mind. Exhausted with fear, Gwen fell asleep as Snow curled up in her arms.

CHAPTER 4
ULTRAVIOLET LIGHT

The next day Gwen was awakened by the whistling wind. The first thing she noticed was the gloomy gray sky left by the previous night's storm. The clouds sprinkled raindrops that speckled the glass. She lay staring off into space and feeling numb. She could still hear Nicholas screaming and moaning in pain.

She remembered how his face changed; how his two eyes merged combining into one. All she could think of was the agony he had to endure locked in a room bound by shackles and chains. Gwen didn't believe the Prince wanted to hurt her. The more she thought about it, the more despondent she became.

At last, the sun emerged from the gray and the rain stopped. Gwen sat up on the bed, crossed her legs, and put her palms on her temples. Snow rubbed against her back before swaying around in front of her. He meowed and head butted her. She kissed his forehead and laid back down. She didn't want to return home but hadn't wanted to leave there either. Locked away in her room, she buried herself under the covers, curled in a fetal position as the hours passed.

In the afternoon Gwen decided to leave her room. When she opened the door, she discovered an envelope at her feet. It had been sealed with a wax and stamped with the letter *N*. She lifted the seal and unfolded the letter:

I have arranged for Charles to take you to your desired destination.

If you so choose and wish to depart, he will ensure your travels are safe. Your carriage awaits.

Best Regards, Nicholas

Gwen held the note in her hand as she walked down the palace steps. She found the main room empty and rushed down a corridor to the castle's front entrance. As she approached the grand, arched doors, two guards opened them for her. She went outside and stood under the still dripping stone. The smell of the wet pavement refreshed her. The sun was shining down, and birds were chirping. Before the castle gates, a coachman was patiently waiting atop a white carriage pulled by Sheamus.

"There you are. All ready to go then?" the man asked.

"No, actually I was looking for Nicholas," she said.

"The Prince? You *want* to see the Prince?"

"Yes, I'd like to have a word with him please. Also, I won't be leaving,"

"Are you quite sure?" he asked.

"Yes." She looked down at the cobblestone. "Yes, I'm sure."

"Very well then, guards!" the man called and clapped his hands.

One of the guards standing by the palace doors ran over to them.

"Yes Charles?" the guard asked.

"This young lady would like to speak to the Prince," the coachman instructed.

"Alright miss, right this way," the guard said with a confused tilt of his head.

"Thank you," Gwen said.

Gwen and the guard returned to the castle and

down the main hall, past the kitchen to the other side of the palace. There they entered another hallway with a window that overlooked the wheat fields. The hall led to a platform of only four steps, the stairs were covered in a royal blue fabric and ended before large dark maple doors guarded by two knights. Her escort nodded to the knights, and they opened the doors for Gwen and her escort to enter.

The throne room was marvelous. The ceiling of the long room was two stories high. The room was decorated in a bright shade of white, royal blue, and antique gold. Radiant sunlight shined through gold framed windows that opened onto the wheat fields. Color portraits of each member of the royal family accentuated the walls. Crystal chandeliers hung from the ceiling. At the end of the room stood another platform in blue. On it sat two golden thrones bedazzled with sapphires and diamonds. On each side of the platform stood marbled white podiums with golden dragon sculptures that reminded Gwen of Leux. The room was filled with rows and rows of white chairs with single blue stripes on the back.

Gwen and the guard remained by the doors beside two podiums with dragons. On the other side of the room stood the Prince and Queen Helena. Gwen was dumbfounded. The Prince looked like his regular self once more. He was his usual height, dressed in royal attire, and had two eyes instead of one.

Gwen didn't understand. She knew what she saw the night before was real and did in fact happen. The image of Nicholas she was looking at was also real. It was as if nothing ever happened.

"We don't know what danger is coming or what disaster awaits this kingdom. We have to be ready to act at all times," the Prince said to the Queen.

"And we are Nicholas. We have knights and guards ready at every door, and walking the allures," the Queen assured him.

As they spoke, Nicholas turned to see Gwen.

"Gwen," he said. "What are you doing here?"

She walked up to the platform. "I was hoping to have a word."

"Are you sure you don't want to go with Charles? You don't have to stay," he replied.

"I'm sure. I'm not ready to leave just yet," she said.

The Queen, head held high, looked from Gwen to her son. She lifted the hem of her dress as she stepped down and walked out of the room. Nicholas left the platform and took a seat in a chair. Gwen cautiously walked over to him but remained standing.

"I know you saw me last night. Really, you don't have to stay. You can leave. It's alright and probably for the best," the Prince told her.

"I just...just...don't understand. What happened to you last night? Why did you turn into... what you did?" Gwen asked still puzzled.

"I'm surprised you want to know. In fact, I'm shocked that you're still here. Please, have a seat wherever you're comfortable. It's a long story."

Gwen pulled out a white chair and sat in front of him. She looked at him ready to listen to what he had to say.

"It was a long time ago. I was young, in my mid-twenties." The Prince lowered his head in shame, wiped his forehead, and sighed "I was cursed by a crone."

Nicholas looked back up at Gwen in embarrassment.

"A crone? Why?" she asked.

"She came to me disguised as a maiden about my age. She magically altered her appearance to look beautiful," he said. "She had long red hair with blue eyes and skin light as snow. She was infatuated with me and lured me in so she could take over the kingdom. When she came to me, I didn't know it was the crone."

"Go on," Gwen said.

"She often came sneaking around outside the castle. She'd knock on my window asking me to come outside. Other times I would follow her into the forest. No matter what she did or how beautiful she was, I just didn't love her. She would try holding my hand and kissing me, but I rejected her advances. This went on for months, but my heart just wasn't with her.

"She wanted to know why I didn't love her. I didn't have an answer, I just didn't. I felt she was trying to manipulate me. She would yell at me and ask me why I wouldn't go with her to the meadow. It was like she was trying to force me.

"I knew something wasn't right. She never wanted to know anything about me. When she came around, no one else ever saw her. They were always doing something else or sleeping. It was strange.

"She was envious of my mother and started watching her. One day I caught her in my mother's room putting on makeup, wearing one of her dresses, and admiring herself in the mirror. I asked her what she was doing. She played it off like everything was fine."

While the Prince told his story, his mind drifted. The past that haunted him returned to replay in his mind

"I'm imagining what it would be like to be your princess someday," the young maiden said, twirling around in a pink ballgown.

She kissed him leaving a crimson print on his cheek.

"You're not going to be my princess," Nicholas said, wiping the lipstick from his face. "I'd like for you to leave. Please go away and don't bother me anymore. I don't love you."

The maiden ran from the room crying, mascara running down her perfect face.

"I'm sorry. I don't want to hurt you," he called after her.

Suddenly, she stopped running and turned to him. Her face seemed to melt as she became the crone once more.

"If you won't make me your princess, then you will no longer be the Prince," the crone said, her voice deep and cruel.

"I just want you to leave me alone," he whimpered.

The Prince slowly backed away, but she pinned him against the wall her face an inch from his. Nicholas desperately reached for his sword. The crone pointed her sharp dirty nail at his eyeball and his hand fell away from the sword.

A violet sphere enveloped the Prince paralyzing him. Together they levitated from the ground. Unable to move, he tried to scream but nothing came out. He floated helplessly while she grinned at him. The crone's eyes shined silver as she began to chant.

"She cursed me," Nicholas said and looked at Gwen.

"That's horrible," Gwen said, her voice sinking.

"After that, she was gone. She disappeared and I fell to the floor. At first, I didn't think she actually did anything. I was still me. It wasn't until the full moon that I started to change. It's been that way ever since."

"I'm so sorry." She placed her hand on his knee. He looked down at it and she quickly drew it back. "I'm not scared of you."

"You should be," he replied.

"I don't think you'll hurt me. I don't think you want to hurt anyone."

"I don't *want* to hurt anyone but that doesn't mean I won't. When..." he sighed and closed his eyes. "When

I turn into the Cyclops, I'm barbaric, a monster. I try my best to control the beast but I'm not sure I always can. That's why I lock myself up."

"I understand and I'm so sorry this happened to you," Gwen told him.

"Don't be. It's my fault. I did this to myself."

"What? How can you say that? It's not your fault at all. The crone was vindictive and spiteful because she didn't get her way. She's evil," Gwen said.

"I am evil. She made me evil when she turned me into a beast."

"I don't believe that. I believe we choose for ourselves who we are and who we want to be. Cyclops or not, you're still Nicholas," Gwen reassured him.

"You really are better off just leaving. Not only is it what's best for your safety but for your sanity as well," the Prince said.

"I'd like to stay awhile longer if that's alright though."

"If you insist. It should be fine now that the full moon is over. That is, until the next one.

"I'll be okay for now. Thank you for letting me stay. And thank you for sharing your story with me." She got up from her chair.

"Gwen?" Nicholas said.

"Yes?"

"If there's anything you need, let someone know."

"I will. Thank you."

Gwen walked from the throne room sighing in distress. As she passed the kitchen and pantry, she spotted a door that led outside. No one was in sight. She slipped through the door into the woods. She hoped to find a place to think. Walking through a grove, inhaling the fresh air, she sat down on a log to think about the Prince. She wanted to help him and break the curse, but she wasn't sure how. After some thought, Gwen shouted for the fairies.

The forest was still and quiet. nothing out of the

ordinary happened.

"Fairies! Fairies!" she called again.

When no answer seemed to come, she laid down on the log wondering where she could find the crone. Suddenly, the air shimmered and Gwen sat up as the fairies appeared.

"You came! I wasn't sure if you heard me or where you were. It's the Prince," Gwen cried.

"The Prince? You met him?" the Quildorra asked.

"Yes, I've been staying at the castle."

"Well, it's probably the safest place."

"He's been cursed by the crone. I want to break the curse and free him," Gwen explained.

The fairies gasped and began blinking out one at a time.

"Wait!" Gwen cried.

"We're sorry Gwen. We can't help you with the crone. She would trap us and have us for lunch," Quildorra told her.

"I understand. Is there anyone who can help? What about Sinnafain?"

"We're sorry Gwen. Please don't endanger us again. If you do, you won't see us anymore," Quildorra said and blinked out.

Only one fairy remained floating on buzzing wings.

"I'm sorry Shadow. I don't know what I was thinking," Gwen said, lowering her head in disappointment.

"It's alright. Don't be sorry. You want to help the Prince," she answered, golden eyes shining. "I don't think Sinnafain can help but maybe she knows someone who can. Good luck Gwen."

The moment the fairy blinked out Sinnafain came into focus before her.

"I knew you were destined for greatness," the maiden spoke.

"I just want to break the curse. Please, what can I do?" Gwen asked.

"You must be careful. Great danger lies ahead. It's not going to be easy," Sinnafain warned.

"I'll take any help I can get. Just point me in the right direction. Where does the crone live?" Gwen asked.

"My dear, you are not prepared to challenge a mage. Especially one as old and powerful as the crone. Perhaps with time but not yet.," She sat on the log beside Gwen.

"What can I do?" Gwen asked.

"My dear, this is only the beginning. If you go alone, you risk death. There are no shortcuts. When it's time, you'll know."

She subtly touched Gwen's face stroking her cheek, smiled and disappeared. Gwen, frustrated, rose from the log and paced back and forth.

"Come on Gwen think. There has to be a way. Grr." she growled.

"Perhaps I can be of assistance," a charming voice said.

Gwen looked around but didn't see anyone.

"Who said that?" she asked.

"Over here," the voice said.

Again, she saw no one.

"You know, I really don't have time for games. If you're not going to help me then go away," Gwen said, growing angry.

"Calm down deary."

An imp dressed in black leather pants, brown boots, and a brown vest appeared. He wore a white long, flared-sleeve shirt beneath the vest. He was leaning against a large cedar tree.

"Who are you?"

"Who am I? Who are you?" he asked.

"I'm Gwen," she replied.

"Pleasure to meet you, Gwen. My name is Bitzelsnick. At your service." The imp took a bow.

The sun's rays shined down through the trees and

leaves danced on the forests floor as the imp stood up straight again. The shifting light highlighted his sparkly green skin, short curly brown hair and eyes as yellow as lemons. As he approached, the bells on his boots tinkled. He was only three feet tall.

"Do you know the crone?" Gwen asked.

"Do I know the crone? Of course, I know the crone. In fact, I know exactly where she lives. Do you want my help?"

"I do! You see, I'm new here so I don't know my way around. It would be great if you would help me."

Bitzelsnick giggled. "Say, why do you want to help the Prince anyway?"

"The Prince has been nothing but kind to me. He came to me when I was in danger. He made sure I was okay and offered me a place to stay. He's under that terrible curse and locks himself away. It's no way for anyone to live," Gwen explained.

"Yes, I see. Hmm, I don't work for free. If I help you, what's in it for me?" he asked.

"Well, what would you like? I can bring you food, clothes, or I can pay you. Do you accept money?" Gwen asked.

"No, no, no," the imp said his voice growing malevolent and shaking his head. "I want much more."

"Okay, Mr. Bitzelsnick, what *do* you want?"

"Bring me the black opal dragon egg from the castle. Then you'll have yourself a deal," he said.

"You want a dragon's egg? Are you out of your mind!" Gwen's eyes widened in shock.

"All magic comes at a price deary," the imp insisted, crossing his arms.

"There has to be something else you would want. Jewels perhaps?"

"I would accept your first-born child or perhaps your head," Bitzelsnick bargained.

"You can't be serious," Gwen complained.

"Oh, but I am deary. I'm very serious. That's my offer. Deal or no deal?" The imp stomped his boot, ringing his bells.

"I don't know. Maybe I'm better off doing this alone," Gwen said, shaking her head.

"You're the one who doesn't know your way around. It's your funeral," Bitzelsnick said.

"Okay fine, the dragon egg it is. You have yourself a deal."

Overjoyed, the imp jumped and kicked his heels together. "Splendid! You have three days to bring me the egg. It mustn't be damaged. Once you hand over the egg, we will seek out the crone and break the curse. Shake my hand to seal the deal." He offered Gwen his small chartreuse hand.

She swallowed her pride and hesitantly took hold of the imp's hand.

"Ow!" she cried, quickly pulling away.

Her palm was bleeding. Bitzelsnick gave Gwen an ardent smile.

"What did you do that for?" she asked holding her hand and looking at the blood.

"You signed the contract. I'll see you in three days. Bring the egg back here to this spot. I will be waiting," Bitzelsnick instructed.

The imp turned back into the forest and disappeared in the shadows. Gwen looked down at her hand to see it was healed. The birds began singing once more as she walked through the bushes on her way back to her room in the castle.

The next morning Gwen awoke determined to snatch the egg. She turned left into the hallway and headed down the spiraling staircase. Looking out of the small windows, she could see the dome of the greenhouse and birds soaring around it. Further down the stairs, she saw the Prince standing in the garden. He mustn't know what she was up. She knew if

Nicholas found out about Bitzelsnick or about her going to the crone, he would undoubtedly forbid it.

She was not about to let him stop her. Her plan was dangerous, but she believed she had nothing left to lose. Her parents, her job, and Daniel were gone. She felt sad for the Prince. She understood how it felt for someone to be cruel and merciless to her. Sitting down on the steps, she looked out the window dispirited. Inside she knew she had to break the curse. She was willing to do whatever it took.

Wiping her tears, she stood and walked down the steps. Gwen thought maybe inside every man was a beast who needed love. While love was not her object, she hoped to restore the Prince's happiness. She reached the bottom of the staircase as Nicholas entered.

"Good morning," he said with a smile.

"Good morning, your majesty," Gwen replied.

"Please, it's Nicholas."

"Very well. Good morning, Nicholas." Gwen smiled back at him.

"Have you had breakfast yet?" he asked.

"No, thank you. I'm not hungry. I was just heading to the kitchen for a cup of tea," she explained.

"I hope you're feeling alright. I *do* apologize again for giving you such a fright."

"Oh, there's no need to apologize. I'm fine, really," Gwen said.

"Alright, well I'm glad," the Prince said as he walked away.

Gwen walked down the long hall to the kitchen. Madeleine was rinsing a basket full of carrots with long green stems. Madeleine was in her overalls with her hair in a single braid that reached down the middle of her back.

"Good morning," Gwen greeted her.

"Good morning," Madeleine said.

"Those carrots look lovely."

"They're just carrots," the gardener said.

"Yes well, how are you this morning?" Gwen asked.

Madeleine took the carrots out of the water and cleaned them off with a rag. Her arms were dirty and wet all the way up to her elbows.

"Tired, I have a lot of work to do. A lot of food has ripened," she explained.

"Would you like some help?" Gwen asked.

"That's quite alright."

She turned around drying her arms and hands with the rag. She added the carrots to a basket of tomatoes, eggplant, and yellow squash. When she left, Gwen found a cup and poured herself some tea. She noticed the honey but didn't want to upset the brownies, so she added a teaspoon of sugar.

Gwen noticed a door next to the kitchen leading to a pantry and went inside. There she found more honey, cream, milk, and mangoes. Gwen took some cream and a mango and carried them into the kitchen. She took a jar of honey, sliced the mango and squeezed the juice into the honey. Taking a dish, she poured some cream, leaving both the cream and honey uncovered on the counter.

"Here's that cream and honey I promised you. I do hope you like it," Gwen called.

She sipped her tea as she looked out the kitchen window on the beautiful summer day. A moment later, she heard Griswald speaking outside the kitchen doors.

"Yes, I will let the Queen know her bath is ready," he said, his voice fading into the background.

A hummingbird was outside the kitchen window. Gwen admired its bright colors for a moment as it flew across the field to sample nectar from a fuchsia flower. Her time was short. Three days would go by fast. She finished her tea, washed her cup and put it back in the cabinet before she left the kitchen.

74

On her way along the hall, she saw the hobs coming up from the dungeon where they had fed the prisoners.

"What's down there?" she asked.

"None of your business. Don't go down there. Stay out," the hob said and snickered.

"Oh, okay," Gwen said and went back up to her room.

In the hall outside she saw the butler. His name escaped her.

"Excuse me, sir?" Gwen asked.

"Yes?"

"Do you, by chance, have any extra sheets for my bed?"

"Oh yes, of course. There's a linen closet down that way. It's all the way at the end on the left. I can get them for you," the butler offered.

"Thank you, you're very kind. Are there perhaps any dark colored ones?" Gwen asked.

"Dark sheets? Oh, my, yes." His cheeks became rosy as he blushed in embarrassment.

"Thank you kindly," Gwen smiled.

The butler went down the hall and brought back a stack of folded black sheets.

"Here you are Miss. Please let me know if there's anything you need that you can't find."

"Thank you. I'm sorry, what was your name again? I apologize but I forgot."

"Gerald, Miss."

"Thank you again Gerald. Oh, and could you bring more food for my cat?"

"Yes of course. I will do that right away," he said.

"Thank you," Gwen said, walking back down the hall.

She closed the bedroom door behind her, wrapped the dark sheet around her and looked out over the balcony at the sea. A moment later, she strolled over to the bookcase, pushed down on a shelf and the case opened. She stepped inside and slowly walked down the steps as quietly as possible. Snow followed close behind her. Hearing only the moaning, whimpering prisoners, she reached the bottom and popped her head around the corner. The men, weak and tired, were sleeping slouched down against the stone.

From the sight and stench, Gwen could tell the hobs never bathed them. Gwen walked by each cell careful not to disturb any of the prisoners. In the last cell, a man with a long, stringy beard and hair like a rat's nest sat looking at the sun.

"Who's there? I can hear you," he said in a weak voice.

Gwen turned her head away. It was dark, and covered in the black sheet, she didn't think he could see her. She kept walking.

"Hi there kitty cat," the frail man said smiling at Snow behind her.

Gwen made her way to the dragon's door. She quietly stepped up to the door and cupped her hand behind her ear. She could hear the dragon snoring. She let out a sigh of relief and looked behind her to make sure the coast was clear before pulling the door open. The shadow was still chained. Gwen made her way inside and the cat followed while the sleeping dragon continued to snore.

Tiptoeing, they were halfway around the dragon when it snarled. Sharp teeth peeked out of its mouth as it slowly opened its violet eyes. Gwen stood still not making the slightest sound. The dragon closed its eyes again and drifted back to sleep. Gwen continued to the long scaly tail to get a full view of the dragon's lair.

It was a tall and dark and dingy cave with piles of bones scattered by the walls. Flow stones draped down over the cave, some smooth and glossy while others were jagged and sharp. There were formations that fused together into columns. Near the dragon's tail, spotlighted by a small ray of light, shimmered a cylinder-shaped object as big as her head that gave off blues and greens.

Gwen knew it was the egg. She stepped cautiously into the space between the tail and the egg. She slowly bent over, picked it up and cradled the egg to her chest. She nervously stepped back over the tail as Snow watched. When the dragon slowly swished its tail, Gwen and Snow took off running.

The dragon arose from its sleep, turned its head and its luminous violet eyes found Gwen. In a rage, the dragon roared. It stomped the chains that held it and ripped them from the ground. Spreading its wings, the dragon started toward her. Gwen looked back and picked up her pace as beams like lasers shot from its purple eyes. Up ahead, Gwen saw a light shining. She clutched the egg tighter and ran as fast as she could. She could feel the heat of the dragon's breath on her back. Jaws snapped behind her and long claws scraped the cave floor. From its open mouth, the dragon released spirals of black glittering smoke.

The shadows quickly spread, almost reaching Gwen. She fell onto the cave floor, the egg cradled in one arm and grabbed Snow pulling him close. She closed her eyes as smoke wafted over her. A spherical shield of vivid blue light suddenly surrounded her, Snow, and the egg. Gwen could see the bright hue as the dragon rushed by. Slowly, she reopened her eyes and saw the blue surrounding her was coming from the egg. She could see the dragon in the distance. It waved its spiked tail, and its eyes continued to glow. It looked at Gwen and roared deep and loud, releasing more black smoke from its mouth.

To her left, she saw a lever. She released Snow who stayed with her inside the blue sphere. Standing up and holding onto the egg, she began walking towards the lever. The radiant blue shield gave off enough light for her to see her way through the sparkling smoke. She grasped the egg in her left hand and reached out with her right feeling for the lever. Pulling it all the way back, lifting the portcullis. The smoke cleared and the blue shield faded away. Gwen looked around but the dragon was nowhere in sight.

"Oh no!" she gasped.

In terror she saw the gate was lifted and heard the distant roaring of the dragon. Its menacing screech echoed across the kingdom. Gwen, being careful with the egg, stood in the middle of the open gate. She and Snow stepped toward the outside watching as the dragon lifted off. Behind her, in the back of the cave, a door opened, and an army of guards swarmed in.

Gwen ran from the cave into the grasslands. The dragon roared again, this time from high in the sky. The army of guards ran out into the field behind her and looked around searching for the dragon.

"Over there!" a guard yelled, pointing to the dragon flying above the sea.

The dragon landed and knights on horses galloped toward it. It planted its claws in the ground and started for them. The horses stopped, some rearing on their hind legs. The knights drew their swords and held them high as the obsidian dragon spread its wings. The men yelled as they charged ready to fight.

The dragon's flared nostrils heaved as it beat its wings creating a wind that knocked the men over. The horses labored to stay upright; their hooves dug deep into the dirt. Knights struggled to hold on as others fell to the ground.

One knight gripped the horn of a saddle. His hand slipped, his shield blew away on the wind and the knight fell to the ground. The horse fell forward, snapping its leg as it hit the grass. The dragon grumbled opening its mouth again and spewed spirals of black glittering smoke. The men stood up and pushed their way through the darkness.

Engulfed in the black smoke that filled their lungs, they tried to run but only a few made it back to the castle.

The castle doors quickly closed behind them and Gwen watched in horror as shadows covered the field in a thick lethal fog. Still carrying the egg, she ran from the cover of the bush where she had taken refuge into the forest. The blue sky turned gray as storm clouds appeared. The dragon circled the castle casting its shadow and waving its long shiny tail.

In the library, the Prince dropped the book he was holding when he spotted the dragon. He ran down the palace stairs as the dragon stomped its foot shaking the ground. A moment later, the Queen came rushing down in a robe and nightgown.

"Nicholas!" she called.

Through the staircase window she could see the dragon standing in the middle of the grass. It lifted its head to the sky releasing another roar and took flight.

"Guards! Signal the horns!" the Queen ordered. "Nicholas, someone released the dragon. Zilliah is free from her cave."

"Mother, I have to go. I have to stop her," the Prince said.

"Nicholas no. You can't," Helena begged.

"Mother, I don't have a choice. If I don't go now, she'll destroy the kingdom."

The Queen looked at him, frightened and worried. She knew her son was right. The Prince's head began to twitch side to side. His clothes ripped and fell to floor as he grew to stand twenty feet tall. His eyes merged into one. The Cyclops, his hazel eye filled with rage, roared and made his way around the corner into the arsenal.

His large, knuckled hands grabbed a double headed ax and stood before the palace. He held the ax at his side and bellowed.

CHAPTER 5
THE CYCLOPS PRINCE

Atop the castle knights stood behind the battlements as horns blew a warning throughout the kingdom. Men readied themselves at every corner of the castle. Zilliah soared overhead casting her giant shadow on the men firing arrows and flaming missiles. She continued to blow smoke filling the nearby woods in a heavy black fog.

In the middle of the woods, Gwen watched the trees turn bare as the darkness spread. She ran with the egg, and Snow dashed along behind her meowing in the dark.

"Come Snow, you can do it," Gwen told him, lifting him onto her shoulder as she ran out of the woods.

Gwen sprinted inside the castle and ran to her room where Snow jumped down. She opened a dresser drawer and carefully placed the egg inside, but the egg wouldn't fit. Gwen got down on the floor, and gently rolled it under her bed. She stood back up and looked out through the glass to see the dragon heading towards the mountains that rose from the sea. Nicholas stomped his feet and ran after the dragon with long strides that shook the earth. His feet left deep prints in the soil. Gwen watched quivering, stunned by the sight of the feral Cyclops.

As the Cyclops drew closer, the dragon screeched, gripping a ledge and leaned over the mountain. It gave a rumbling growl as a luminescent violet light arose in its throat. Zilliah lifted her head

releasing cones of smoke into the sky. Lightning
flashed illuminating her ultraviolet eyes as the
Cyclops Prince reached the foot of the mountain. He
began pulling himself up with his giant hands.

Gwen threw open the balcony doors and rushed
to the rail. "Nicholas!" she cried.

The Cyclops turned his head and looked at her.
His one eye glimmered and he gave a roar of rage. He
was just below the dragon. Zilliah swiped at him and
debris crashed onto the shore. The dragon spit her
toxic smoke.

The Cyclops grunted and pulled himself up to
stand beside the dragon. Zilliah roared and started
climbing up the side of another mountain and began
becoming invisible. The Cyclops yelled in a fit of
rage, grabbing the dragon by her leg pulling her
back down. The Cyclops lifted his ax, and the
dragon struck him in the eye.

The Prince moaned in pain as Zilliah's claw sliced
his eye socket. She pulled her arm back and the
Cyclops's eye dangled down the side of his face. The
dragon clawed at the Cyclops's face again, ripping
his eye out in a shower of yellow liquid.

The smoke began draining Nicholas of his
vitality. He stumbled around uneasy as the lightning
flashed. Tracking the dragon by sound, the Cyclops
grabbed the dragon by the neck. Zilliah wailed as the
Cyclops swung onto its back. Bucking to throw
Nicolas off, she dipped and twisted. He gripped both
sides of the dragon's neck tighter as he stood up on
its back.

He snapped the dragon's neck and jumped off
onto the mountain as she slid over the edge. Zilliah
was still alive. She dug her claws into the stone,
lifting herself back up snarling. The Cyclops hoisted
his ax and swung. He roared and swung again.
Blood dripped down his cheeks as Zilliah's head

rolled away. The dragon's body slipped off of the ledge and splashed into the sea.

Back on the mountain, the Cyclops fell to his knees. The Prince grew weaker, his face and skin grew wrinkled. He was quickly aging and collapsed upon the mountain. The black smoke lingered as he lay there on the cold stone, pale and fragile, and he changed back into the Prince. The eyes returned to his face. One was only a gauged-out bleeding socket. His hair became dull and gray, his body shriveled.

Rain began to fall clearing the smoke as the sun set. The dragon's headless body washed up on the shore. Something emerged from the dragon's neck giving off a soft glow that faded in and out. Orbs, the souls of those the dragon had devoured, floated from the dragon changing color from white to blue to violet. They hovered above the body and drifted off into the dead forest floating. As they left Zilliah, the dragon turned into shadow and ash which drifted off in the wind.

It was hard for Gwen to watch. She knew something was wrong when she no longer saw the Prince.

"Nicholas!" she shouted, her cries echoing through the mountains where the Prince lay. "Nicholas!"

She burst into tears, ran back into her room, and out the door.

"Help, somebody help," Gwen cried. "We need to send someone to the mountains for Nicolas."

Gwen ran out of the castle into the rain. As she rushed past the gargoyles their eyes glowed like aquamarines. She made her way past the greenhouse as the downpour splattered on the glass. As Gwen approached the mountains, she called the Prince's name again. Behind her a group of knights appeared galloping on horses.

"He's up on the mountain!" Gwen cried.

"Stay here, don't move," the man ordered.

"No, I'm coming with you!" Gwen shouted.

"It's better if you stay here and out of our way," another guard said as three more men galloped past her.

"Maybe you should get out of my way," Gwen ordered.

"She's a fool. This way," the guard said.

The men made their way toward the mountains. Gwen placed her fingers inside her mouth and whistled. A moment later, she heard the swooshing of something flying. She looked up and from behind the mountains, Leux appeared, golden wings spread wide. He roared answering Gwen's call and landed before her. The brilliant gold dragon narrowed its ruby eyes and lowered itself to the ground. Gwen leaped up on its back.

"Take me to the top of that mountain," Gwen said, pointing the direction she wanted Leux to take her.

The dragon flapped its wings taking flight. It rushed around the greenhouse and landed smoothly on the mountain top. Gwen got off as thunder cracked. Her vision was obscured in the darkness, but she saw an old man lying on the ground.

"Nicholas!" she called unsure if it was him.

The Prince was weak and barely breathing.

"Nicholas! No! It can't be!" she cried, rushing to his side and falling to her knees.

"Nicholas are you alright?" she asked.

The Prince could barely speak. He laid there whimpering and disoriented.

"Leux!" Gwen called. "Leux come, help!"

The dragon gave a low rumble as he approached over the ground stained with blood. Gwen took Nicholas in her arms as she wept.

"I'm so sorry Nicholas. I'm so sorry," she cried, her voice cracking. "We have to get you back to the castle."

The gold dragon lowered itself and Gwen lifted the Prince onto the dragon's back. She climbed up behind him as three knights appeared on their steeds

The dragon stood when they dismounted and drew their swords. Leux hovered above them for a moment before soaring into the night sky. Leux slowly landed before the castle doors and sat on the ground. Gwen got off as two knights ran out into the rain.

"Get the Prince," one knight commanded.

The men slowly pulled Nicholas down. Something was wrong an elderly man was laid on the ground.

"Wait, that's not the Prince," a knight shouted.

"Who is this you foolish girl? An impostor?" another questioned.

"No, I wouldn't. This is the Prince, I swear it," Gwen assured them.

The second knight took a closer look at the old man.

"The girl tells the truth. This is indeed the Prince," he declared.

Leux gave a wild roar. The two knights quickly backed away and drew their swords.

"Hey now. Take it easy!" a knight yelled.

The gold dragon growled again and blew a swirling wind from its mouth that lifted the Prince in the air. Leux's red eyes cast a glow that restored Nicolas' body. When the wind stopped, Nicholas stood up, returned to his proper age. The dragon licked Nicholas's injured eye scarring it over. The Prince began to walk toward the doors and fell. The two knights rushed to pick up the still weak Nicholas.

Gwen hugged the dragon and stroked his face. Leux tilted his head in adoration before pulling away. His golden scales shimmered as he took flight back to the Dragon Lands. Gwen entered the castle and found the room where the Prince was sitting. Gerald brought blankets which the hobs took and covered the shivering Nicholas. Griswald lit a fire in the fireplace.

"Here, drink this," Madeleine said, handing him a mug of steaming tea.

The Prince's hands shook as he took the cup slowly lifting it to his mouth.

"Careful, it's hot," she warned.

"What is this?" he asked after taking a sip.

"Green tea with chamomile and ginger," she replied.

"Thank you." he said, shivering anew.

When she nodded and left the room, a hob took a washcloth dipping it in a bowl of hot water.

"Let's get you washed up," the hob said.

The hobgoblin gently washed the dirt off of the Prince as the logs in the fireplace cracked and popped, sending gold and orange embers up the chimney. The Prince looked better but was still weak as he breathed in the steam rising from the tea.

"My ax? Where's my ax?" Nicholas asked.

"We'll send someone to retrieve it for you, your Highness," a hob said.

The Prince waved his hand, the hob left, and another hob appeared to stand before Nicholas. With a green hand, he lifted the Prince's eyelid. Nicholas drooped as if he were about to pass out.

"Follow my finger," the hob instructed, moving it side to side, then up and down. "How's your head?"

"I'm fine," Nicholas muttered, paused and added, "that dragon better not come back."

"Do you have a headache? Does it hurt or throb?" the hob asked.

"It's nothing some spirits can't cure. You!" the Prince shouted pointing to the other hob. "Bring me some whiskey."

"Your majesty, I believe you have a concussion. You appear to have taken a blow to the head. More than likely when the dragon swiped your eye," the hob said.

"My eye? What about my eye? My eye is fine." the Prince assured him.

The hob looked at his fellow hob and shook his head.

"I'm sorry your majesty but no spirits for you tonight," the hob said.

"No spirits? I don't need your permission. I want whiskey and I want it now," the Prince demanded.

"I'm sorry your Highness. We must take you to your room so you can rest," the hob said.

"Whiskey later then," the Prince said.

"Yes, your Majesty, whiskey and spirits later. Now, let's get you to your room." The butler walked over, placed his arm under Nicholas, and lifted him from the sofa.

"I can walk," the Prince insisted.

"Are you sure?" Gerald asked, slowly releasing Nicholas who took a few stumbling steps. "Let us help you your Majesty."

Assisted by the butler, the Prince slowly approached the staircase.

"It's a long way up and a lot of stairs. We can go slow," Gerald explained.

"Nonsense, I can walk just fine," the Prince replied.

As they began climbing the staircase, Griswald approached. "Sir, your ax," he said.

Griswald looked up at the Prince and lifted the double headed ax offering it to Nicholas. It was dirty, covered with dried mud and Zilliah's blood. The Prince grumbled and took it from him.

"Thank you," the Prince said.

"Of course, your Majesty. Now please, go rest. Ring the bell if you need anything."

"I will," the Prince said.

On the other side of the castle, Gwen returned to her room. Snow meowed and rubbed against Gwen's legs. When she bent down to pick him up, he leaped into her arms and purred. She placed Snow on the bed and kneeled down looking under the bed for the egg.

It was gone.

Gwen searched the room in a panic, digging through the dresser drawers and nightstands. She looked behind the furniture, checked behind the door, and then looked under the bed again. The egg was nowhere to be found.

"Where could it have gone?" she asked.

She checked behind the curtains; bent down to look under a chair. She then rummaged through the closet, throwing the clothes out behind her. There was no egg. It was gone.

"Oh no. What am I going to do?"

Gwen fell back onto the bed. Time was running out. She knew she had to deliver the egg to Bitzelsnick soon.

"If that egg is lost, it's all over. How will I find the Crone and defeat her?"

It was getting dark. She decided to search the rest of the castle. Leaving her room, she went out into the empty hallway. She paused for a moment trying to decide where to start when a mischievous voice spoke.

"Looooking for thisss?"

Gwen spun around to see a brownie with the egg.

"You give that back right now!" Gwen demanded.

"Now why would I do that? You stole our honey. Now, I'm stealing your egg," Harold said.

"I didn't steal your honey. I apologized and I brought you more honey. Now give it back," Gwen demanded.

"Stealing is stealing. And you're a thief," the brownie said.

"You don't understand. I need that egg," Gwen said.

"Catch me if you can," the brownie said and ran rolling the egg in front of him.

"Hey, stop! Come back here!" Gwen called.

The brownie raced down the hall with Gwen in pursuit. Harold reached the end of the hall and approached the staircase.

"No!" Gwen shrieked.

Harold and the egg stopped at the top of the stairs. Gwen, hands on her knees, paused breathing heavily.

"Please, don't."

"You'll never catch me," the brownie shouted, rocking the egg back and forth. It wobbled over the ledge and went tumbling down the stairs.

"Oops," he said rushing down the staircase as Gwen followed.

The egg hit the steps, bounced, flew over the remaining steps onto the marble floor, and rolled down the main hall. As Gwen and the brownie reached the bottom of the staircase, the egg crashed into the Queen's statue and came to a halt.

"Oh, thank goodness," she sighed in relief.

Harold rushed toward the egg, grunting as he struggled to pick it up. He finally got it into his arms.

"Now, can I please have that back?" Gwen asked.

"No, never. It's mine." The brownie's stick legs wobbled under the weight of the egg.

"How about a bargain then?" Gwen asked.

"What kind of bargain?"

"Well, did you try the honey I left you?" she asked.

"No, why would I? For all I know, you could be trying to poison us," the brownie said.

"Poison you? I would never do that," Gwen assured him.

"We already told you; we don't trust you humans. I have what I want right here," he said, rubbing the egg.

"It's okay. Please, calm down. I told you I don't mean you any harm. I meant what I said," Gwen told him.

"You came into this house. You stole our honey. You released the dragon. And you stole the dragon's egg. We will never trust you!" the brownie shouted, steam blowing out his pointy ears.

"No, it's not like that. You don't understand," Gwen answered.

"Trust me, I understand just fine. Leave this castle. We don't want you here," Harold said, his face turning a bright cherry red.

"You're not friendly creatures, are you?" Gwen said.

She went into the kitchen where she found a small spoon, scooped up some of the mango honey and walked back to the brownie. Harold began making a run for it.

"Oh no, you don't," Gwen said, grabbing the scruff of Harold's shirt and lifting him kicking and screaming.

"Let me go!" he demanded, blowing more steam from his ears.

Gwen took the spoon of honey and held it to Harold's mouth.

"I'm not eating that," he said, locking his mouth and lips.

"Come on. Open up," Gwen commanded.

The brownie whimpered and continued to kick his legs as Gwen smeared the honey over his lips. The steam stopped blowing from his ears and his apple red face quickly returned to peach.

"Mmm," he said.

Gwen slowly placed Harold back on the ground. He released his hold on the egg dropping it.

"Okay, you can have the egg. Just give me more of that honey. That is the most delicious honey I've ever had," the brownie said.

Gwen giggled and smiled. "It's the same honey I left you. There's a whole jar of it waiting for you in the kitchen."

"Okay, I'm sorry I took the egg. I take back what I said. You can stay as long as you keep bringing us more of that honey," the brownie said.

"You have a deal, Harold," Gwen replied.

She offered the brownie her finger. Harold took it in his small hand and shook it. Gwen picked up the egg and slowly turned it over. There didn't appear to be any cracks. Gwen took a deep breath and sighed in relief.

Harold returned to the kitchen. He began jumping, trying to grab the cabinet, but he kept falling short. Gwen, hearing the brownie grunting in the other room, walked through the swinging doors.

"Here, let me help you," she offered.

She laid the back of her hand flat on the ground and the brownie stepped over her fingers to stand in her palm. Gwen slowly stood up lifting Harold onto the counter. He ran to the waiting jar of honey. Gwen twisted off the lid and he climbed to the top. Harold took his hand and greedily scooped up the honey.

Gwen took the egg up the staircase that led to the Prince's room. She slowly turned the knob. The Prince was sound asleep. Cradling the egg in one arm, she gently brushed Nicholas's cheek, leaned in, closed her eyes, and kissed him on the forehead. He was safe and come tomorrow, the Prince would never be a Cyclops again. Before walking out of the room, she looked back at Nicholas. He appeared calm. She smiled as she slowly closed the door and made her way back to her room.

CHAPTER 6
REGENERATE

When Gwen awoke the next morning, the grass outside the castle was burned and dead. The trees were bare, their branches broken and dangling. The birds were silent. The magnificence Gwen had come to know was gone. The forest had lost its magic, even the sky was gray and gloomy. Gwen felt numb as she stared blankly at the scene. Opening her door, she found a black dress waiting for her. Gwen put on the long, satin dress with flared sleeves, a hood, and lace corset. There was a ribbon tied in a bow in front. She pulled up the hood and headed downstairs.

In the main hall, all was quiet. The Prince, the Queen, Griswald, Charles, and everyone in the castle were dressed in black. The Prince, looking rough, wore a black silk patch over his scarred eye, his face expressionless.

"We lost some good soldiers yesterday. They were more than just knights and guards, they were good men," he said in a somber tone. "Zilliah was released from the dungeon. The broken portcullis is currently under repair. Thank you, hobs. We also lost some of our most loyal steeds. Today we say our mournful goodbyes. If you would, please form a line and follow me to the chapel to pay our respects."

As they followed the Prince, everyone bowed their heads and wept. The Queen sniffled and dried her tears with a handkerchief. Griswald stared at the ground inconsolable. The Prince led the group over the drawbridge to the gate tower, up the stone stairs, and into the castle's cathedral.

The cathedral ceiling soared over their heads; the walls were supported by great pillars. Painted on the curved ceiling was a mural of cherubs, clouds, and doves. Everything inside was white, blue, or covered in real gold, including the angels in the stained-glass windows. Rows of wooden chairs lined each side of the aisle. Behind the altar stood two tall white angel sculptures. White candles arranged below the name of each knight, guard, and steed dripped wax.

As Gwen read the names, her heart sank, and her eyes filled with tears. She read the horses' names hoping she wouldn't read Sheamus. She felt responsible for every life lost, her pale face filled with remorse and shame. When she paused to read Russ' name, the Prince stopped beside her.

"I'm so sorry Nicholas. This never should have happened," Gwen said.

Sorrow was etched on his face. "It didn't have to be this way. They will all be missed," he replied, lowering his head.

"I'm sorry for your loss. They are all heroes," she said.

Nicholas looked at her but didn't speak. Gwen returned his gaze. She wanted to say something, but the words wouldn't come. He walked to stand before the name of a guard. *Peter,* the plaque said. Nicholas placed his hand on the plaque and gazed at the name.

"Goodbye my dear friend," he whispered.

Everyone there mourned for someone they would never forget. As they wept, a shining gold tail flew by one of the windows. Hobs and halflings hurried out to see what was happening and everyone followed. Leux was spinning in the air. He dipped and soared, blowing life into the land. The dragon's chest glowed with a bright white light that radiated from his mouth. He blasted the air, and a twister appeared to mend the broken branches. The trees sprouted leaves. The lavender fields bloomed, and stumps became trees. The woodlands were green again. Apple blossoms covered the trees with pink petals. The birds resumed their chirping and snuggled in their nests.

Leux soared over the greenhouse and around the garden to touch down in front of the gate tower. The crowd stared with amazement at the restored landscape and knights drew their swords in a salute. Nicholas stepped forward looking up at the dragon whose golden scales shimmered in the sunlight. The dragon locked gazes with the Prince and the ground trembled.

Leux roared and a cloud encompassed the dragon hiding him from view. As it slowly dissipated, two bare feet appeared. The dragon had become a man. The wind stirred his long white hair and beard. He wore a blue cloak with gold stars and had a tall, pointed hat to match. The man shook his arm, and a wooden quarterstaff appeared in his hand. Gold swirled around the large blue topaz at its tip. The man looked at the Prince with a crooked smile.

"Leux, my old friend. It's so nice to see you," the Prince said, offering his hand.

"Prince Nicholas, a pleasure as always," the man replied, exchanging a firm handshake.

"Everyone, this is Leuxandol, the wizard. He's a dear friend. Please, welcome him." Nicholas smiled and patted the wizard on the back.

"You can just call me Leux," the wizard said with a grin as they approached the group.

Gwen watched Leux, frozen with awe.

"You must be Gwen," he said, lifting his hat, and bowing his head.

"Leux?"

"Yes, a pleasure to formally meet you," he answered, smiling.

"I... I... just can't believe it's really you."

"Yes of course it's me. Don't look so surprised," the wizard said with an amused chuckle.

"Old friend, join me in the castle for some rum," the Prince insisted.

"That does sound nice," Leux replied.

"The pleasure's all mine," Nicholas said with a laugh.

While they made their way to the solarium to share laughter and a drink, Gwen snuck back to her room and retrieved the black opal egg from under her bed. She turned the egg over rubbing its scales to ensure it wasn't damaged. It appeared intact but as she held it, the egg began to shake.

"Oh, please wait until I deliver you to Bitzelsnick before you hatch," she pleaded.

She placed the egg on the bed and pulled a purple knitted blanket from the dresser. Swaddling the egg in her arms, she pulled her hood up to hide her face and opened the bookcase. She walked down the steps and heard the voices of the hobs repairing the portcullis in the dungeon.

"Ah, it's still broken. Turn it this way while I pull," a hob said.

Gwen turned right and pushed open a heavy door that led outside. She looked both ways and hurried out onto the grass. She pulled her hood closer to her face and carried the egg toward the woods searching for the cedar tree. She soon spotted the tree and lowered her hood.

There it is, she thought, rushing to it while cicadas buzzed around her.

"Bitzelsnick," Gwen called, holding the egg to her chest.

The wind ruffling the leaves was the only answer.

"Bitzelsnick, where are you?" she called.

Glowing orange embers filled the air, burning in bright shades of yellow and red. The swirling embers gathered in the air and the imp stepped from them.

"There you are deary. Hmm, looks like you're right on time. Lucky you. Do you have my egg?" he asked, stepping forward into the sun.

"I have the egg right here. Remember our deal. As soon as I hand it over, you have to help me with the crone," Gwen reminded him.

"Why yes. Of course, I do. We signed a contract after all."

"Good. I'm not sure if this is the right thing to do. I don't think the dragon inside is evil," Gwen said.

"A deal is a deal, deary."

"What are you going to do with the egg?" Gwen asked.

"Ah, I should have had you sign a non-disclosure too. It's none of your business what I do with the egg. All that matters is that you stick to our agreement and hand it over," Bitzelsnick demanded.

"How do I know this dragon isn't good?" Gwen asked.

"It came from the shadow dragon, didn't it?" the imp asked.

"Well yes."

"Then this is likely a shadow hatchling. Rest assured these dragons are evil. It will grow up like its mother. Handing the egg over to me, you'll never have to worry about the creature harming anyone ever again," Bitzelsnick assured her.

"Well, I guess you're right. It probably is for the best," Gwen said.

"Thank you deary, now hand over the egg."

Gwen unwrapped the egg and held it out to Bitzelsnick. The imp examined it in the light.

"Well, deary, it doesn't appear to be damaged. Congratulations, you succeeded. You can keep your first-born child, *and* I will help you find the crone," Bitzelsnick said.

"It wasn't an easy task, and I feel awful for all the damage Zilliah caused. But now, the Prince can be free," Gwen said.

Bitzelsnick giggled and the egg started shaking again. The shaking increased until the shell finally cracked.

"I take it back. No deal. The egg is hatching," the imp shouted, laying the egg on the ground.

Bitzelsnick put his hands on top of his head and ran around in circles in a panic.

"No, we had a deal. I delivered the egg to you undamaged. You inspected it and said it was to your liking. It's too late now. A deal is a deal," Gwen insisted.

The imp stopped running. As they watched a piece of the shell broke off. A blue hatchling looked out at them with big golden eyes.

"That's not a shadow dragon. You lied to me," Gwen said.

"I didn't lie. I said it was likely. I was just wrong, that's all," the imp countered.

The egg broke into pieces leaving the blue baby dragon on the ground. Its scales shone and there were golden marks under its wings and belly. It had a horn atop its snout. The hatchling yawned and grumbled. The imp ran up to the baby, took his long sharp nail, and sliced the hatchling's neck open. Ravenous, Bitzelsnick drank the dragon's blood.

"Hey, what did you do that for? It's not a shadow dragon," Gwen shouted.

The imp gulped the last of its blood, turned his head, and looked back at Gwen blood dripping from his mouth.

"Blue dragons are evil too," he said.

The dragon turned purple, then back to blue. For a moment the hatchling became translucent. Gwen squinted her eyes concentrating on the baby dragon. The hatchling's head sparked with electricity.

"I can't watch this," Gwen said, covering her eyes.

A moment later, a bush rustled, and Gwen opened her eyes to look. Snow ran out to her.

"Snow, how did you find me?" she asked.

Then, she remembered she had forgotten to close the bookcase.

"Oh, Snow," she said as the cat looked up purring.

"Ready to go find the crone?" Bitzelsnick asked.

Gwen covered her eyes again.

"It's okay deary, you can uncover your eyes. There's nothing more to see," he said.

Gwen spread her fingers and peeked between them. The dragon and the egg were gone.

"Where did the dragon go?" she asked.

"It was scrumptious," Bitzelsnick said. "Now, to find the crone. Follow me, deary."

The imp smiled and started walking. Gwen, with Snow alongside her, followed him through the forest. The forest grew darker as they went. Luna moths flew by, their fluorescent wings glimmering. Nearer the marshes, dragonflies soared over the water, buzzing as the sky was smeared in pink and orange. The trees were covered in Spanish moss and a lingering mist coated the ground. Snow leaped into Gwen's arms to avoid the bogs.

"Stay close and don't stray," Bitzelsnick whispered.

His little body jolted; sparks popped from his head. When they did, Gwen slipped and fell into a pile of sludge. Snow jumped onto the imp's shoulder with a meow. Gwen was covered head to toe in goop. She tried to get up, slipped, and fell on her rear. She slowly got up, her dress was dripping and her wet shoes squeaked. She lifted her feet one at a time to remove her shoes.

"Oh deary, that isn't a good look for you," the imp said with a snicker. "Hold still."

He reached into his pocket and took out a wand, twirled it in the air, and pointed it at Gwen. The tip glowed a bright yellow and she was clean and dry.

"Put your shoes back on, deary," Bitzelsnick told her.

"Thank you, fairy godmother," Gwen replied, slipping her shoes back on.

"Watch where you step from now on, would you," the imp warned.

They continued through the swamp guided by pale moonlight. They walked beneath a tree and vultures hissed at them.

"Ah, vultures, we're getting close," Bitzelsnick said.

The moon didn't seem to move, and the sky was still. A long dark snake slithered past her feet. She looked down at the cottonmouth and froze in fear. Bitzelsnick and Snow kept walking while the snake slithered up a tree.

"Uhhhh, Bitzelsnick," Gwen said.

"What is it deary?"

"Are you sure we're going the right way? I think I've seen this tree before. Are we lost?"

"Lost? Shhhhh, don't say anything," he whispered, pulling a compass from his pocket.

"Are you okay?" Gwen asked.

"I'm fine deary."

As he spoke, a bolt of lightning flew from his mouth. Gwen ducked and it hit a tree snapping a branch in half. The imp giggled covering his mouth.

"Oops, just my lunch, that's all," he said, moving behind a bush. "Get down."

When Gwen knelt, her shoulder rubbed against the imp, and she got a shock. Bitzelsnick parted the leaves revealing a light gray cottage with a brown thatched roof.

"This is it. This is where the crone lives. Her home only appears by magic. That's why you thought we were going in circles. I am an arcane master after all." Bitzelsnick snickered.

Bitzelsnick waved his wand, and it transformed into a lantern.

"Whatever you do, do not wake the crone. "Wait here."

"No, it's too dark. I won't be able to see anything. We came all this way; I have to do this."

"It's too dangerous. The cottage is protected by her magic. There are traps all around, you just can't see them," he told her.

"I'm not afraid," Gwen said.

"Maybe not but I'm small and I know how to avoid the traps. You want to help? Keep watch and be ready."

"Okay fine," Gwen replied, lifting Snow from his shoulder.

"Just stay here," the imp insisted.

He scurried down the pebble path and slowly approached a side window. He lifted it up and looked back at Gwen. When he did, the crone's hands came through the window and snatched the imp inside. The window and shutters slammed shut.

"Oh no, Bitzelsnick," Gwen cried.

Inside, the cottage was dark with dreary walls of stone. On the hearth, before a long wooden table, a fire burned beneath a cauldron. A dusty old besom leaned against the wall nearby.

"I didn't know I was having imp for dinner," the crone said, her breath reeking of sulfur.

Behind the table was a counter filled with labeled jars: *mug wort, graveyard dirt, coffin nails, and snakeskin.* Next to the fireplace were shelves covered with dusty bottles of potions.

"I'm not here to be stew wench. I'm here to slay you," Bitzelsnick announced.

The crone's long stringy gray hair swayed as she cackled in reply. She grabbed Bitzelsnick by the waist and the imp pushed himself forward, bit off a chunk of her ear, and spit it out. She shrieked in pain and dropped him. Bitzelsnick ran toward the lantern on the floor, and it turned back into his wand.

"Come little imp. I have a warm bath waiting for you," she said with a sweet old lady voice.

Bitzelsnick jumped onto the table, ran across it, and leaped to grab a chandelier. The flames dipped and danced as the imp swung in the air.

"Get down from there this instant. You're being a real pain in my keister," the crone scolded.

Bitzelsnick kicked his legs back and forth swinging harder. He let go of the chandelier, flew through the air, and latched onto the crone's face. She stumbled backward and grabbed Bitzelsnick trying to pull him off her. When she managed to pull him away, two of his sharp claws gouged her eyes out. She screamed in pain. Bitzelsnick hit the table and jumped across it landing on the shelves with the potions. He quickly searched the labels: *llama, sheep, toad, love spell, nightmares, raise the dead* and smashed them on the floor. The crone stumbled blindly, bumped into the cauldron, slipped and fell onto the floor, yellow liquid splashing on her head. She screamed in agony as the liquid blistered her skin. Her face swelled, her cheeks turned blue, and her fingers turned black.

Bitzelsnick continued throwing more potions. *Vampire, Spider, Lich, Hex Breaker.* He put the *Hex Breaker* in his pocket. Beneath the screaming crone, the floor smoked pink, red, and purple. Her eyes suddenly regenerated, and her wailing ceased. Her arms and hands sprouted black hair. She grew legs until she had eight but remained unchanged from the waist up. Her eyes glowed like fiery embers and multiplied into the eight crimson orbs of a giant black widow. Bitzelsnick jumped down from the shelves and ran for the door as the crone scampered on her long arachnid legs after him.

He jumped for the knob, turned it, and ran out of the cottage. In the doorway, she reared up on her four hind legs and thousands of tiny black widows rushed through the cottage door chasing Bitzelsnick. He ran through a shimmering veil before him and bolted past Gwen who quickly turned and followed him. The crone broke through the veil a moment later and her spiders scattered over the rocks.

"Gwen, take my hand!" Bitzelsnick yelled.

Gwen reached for the imp holding Snow close with her other arm. Gwen gripped the imp's hand, and they blinked out of the swamp to reappear in the forest by the ancient cedar tree.

CHAPTER 7
SHATTERED GLASS

Gwen and Bitzelsnick stood shaking in the place where they materialized once more. The sun was setting above the forest. Bitzelsnick reached into his pocket and pulled out a cylinder-shaped black bottle, holding the cork between this thumb and middle finger. The label read *Hex Breaker*.

"This is what you need right here, deary. Add three drops to the prince's drink on the night of the full moon. Everything magical happens in a set of threes. Do this before midnight and the curse will be broken," the imp said.

"Is that it? Isn't there anything else I need to do?" Gwen asked.

"Make sure he finishes every last drop. The potion is yours now deary--catch!" Bitzelsnick shouted, tossing the potion in the air.

Gwen dove to catch it. The bottle fell into her hands, and she landed on her stomach.

"Thank you Bitzelsnick."

When she looked up, the imp was gone. She stood, wiping the dirt from her dress. There was no one around except her and Snow. As owls hooted and insects buzzed, they stood there wondering what to do.

Snow looked up at the crescent moon shining down through an opening in the trees and blinked his sapphire eyes. He meowed and Gwen bent over to pick him up. He wrapped his paws around her neck, purring as he looked up at the twinkling stars.

Gwen walked out of the forest and across lavender fields as a gentle gust of wind blew in from the sea. Gwen snuck back inside the castle through a side door. She made her way up the stairs and stepped through the bookcase into her room, closing it behind her and placing Snow on the floor. She put the potion inside the nightstand next to her bed and lay down to look out at the calm night. Happy in the knowledge that soon the Prince would be free of his pain, a big, bright smile swept across her face. She got up and walked to the window to look at the moon and wonder when it would be full.

***

Not all was as peaceful as it seemed from her window. In the swamp, the crone was spinning webs and weaving nests. Her spiders stayed close. They worshipped her as their queen, while dangling from nearby trees on silken webs watching her build a sanctuary for them.

Nearby, a young man, named Thomas, hummed as he wandered through the forest.

Which way is home?

Thomas wasn't large man by any means. His thin frame stood only five feet four inches tall. He had short blond hair swooped over to the side above blue eyes. The young man had walked for hours and had grown tired.

"Hello," he called in hopes that someone would hear him.

When nothing but the quiet woods answered, he continued on his way, still humming as he went.

"Ah!" he squealed when a spider suddenly dropped onto his shoulder.

He quickly wiped the black widow onto the ground. He soon found himself surrounded by intricate webs and standing in the middle of what appeared to be a giant cocoon. His eyes widened in terror as more spiders appeared.

"Spi...spi...spi...spiders," he stammered.

Thomas froze, paralyzed by fear, as the crone slowly emerged from her cocoon. One by one her eight legs reached the ground. Nests ripped open spilling thousands of baby spiders that rushed towards the young man. They infested his legs. He aggressively wiped them away

"Oh my god spiders. Get off of me," he whimpered.

As the crone sprinted toward him, he turned and fled.

"Spiders!" he screamed, running into the night. "Help! Help!"

The army of black widows swarmed over the swamp, making their way beyond the mangroves as Thomas splashed across the bogs ahead of them. He ran, still screaming, until he was out of the woods. He reached the castle door at last and pounded on the door.

"Help! Please! Somebody help!" he cried, banging on the wood with both fists. The door opened with a loud creaking sound.

"What's the meaning of this?" the guard asked.

At the edge of the forest, the crone stood up on her back legs and wailed. The young man frantically pushed his way inside.

"Spiders...giant spiders."

At the sound of his voice another guard ran out of a room at the top of the stairs.

"Thomas? Is that you?" the guard asked.

"Dad," Thomas cried.

His father, wearing a black robe, ran down the palace steps to embrace his son. "What seems to be the problem?"

"I got lost and couldn't find my way back. I was attacked by spiders," Thomas said, breathing heavily.

"Well, you're alright now. Come, we'll find you a room." his father said.

***

At dawn, Gwen oblivious that the crone was on the prowl, awoke to the birds chirping in their nests. She lay in bed while Snow headbutted her purring and she held him close, as he kneaded her with his paws.

The castle outside her room grew noisy. She could hear talking, laughing, and the sounds of pots and pans banging far away. Gwen changed into her mauve dress and left her room. Going down the steps, hobs walked by carrying platters. When Gwen reached the bottom, another hob rushed past her.

"Coming through!" the hob said.

Madeleine, carrying a basket full of vegetables, walked past Gwen taking beets and onions to the kitchen.

"Pardon me," the gardener said.

"Good morning," Gwen replied.

"There's breakfast being served in the dining room if you're hungry!" Madeleine announced, passing Gwen and entering the kitchen.

Gwen walked into the dining room where knights, guards, halflings, and hobs were all enjoying their morning feast. The room filled with chatter as they sipped coffee, broke brown bread, and ate scrambled eggs. The Prince and the Queen were both absent. The room was filled with all the tenants. Gwen found herself in a seat next to Griswald.

"Good morning," Gwen smirked, sitting in the chair.

"Good morning, Gwen," Griswald answered, reaching for a plate of butter.

"Coffee or tea?" a female halfling with curly blonde locks asked Gwen.

"Tea please," Gwen answered.

The halfling poured the hot liquid into a teacup.
Across the table, an introverted halfling held a book
open in his hairy hand. While reading it and sipping
his coffee. His hair peeked around his ears and gold
rimmed reading glasses sat on the tip of his nose. A
hob placed a platter before Gwen and removed the lid.
She spread butter over the brown bread and topped it
with eggs. She added a spoonful of sugar to her
steaming tea and stirred it.

Gwen looked and saw a young man at the end of
the table she had never seen before. He was sitting
with a guard. She learned his name was Thomas and
the guard was his father. She thought nothing of it at
the time. She continued eating her breakfast,
wondering when the next full moon would be and how
she would sneak the potion into the Prince's drink.

When she finished, Gwen rose from her chair,
pushed it in and left the dining room. Something was
off though. Things didn't seem quite right to her. She
wrinkled her forehead and glanced at the marbled
floor. She couldn't help but feel someone was watching
her. As she walked away, the chatter faded into the
background. Gwen walked out of the castle for some
fresh air.

She went to the stables in search of Sheamus. She
found him at the far end of the stalls.

"Hello Sheamus," Gwen greeted him with a smile.
"I'm glad you're okay."

The horse stepped closer and placed his snout in
Gwen's hand. She brushed him affectionately.

"Hey, you can't be in here!" a guard shouted.

Gwen turned towards him. "I'm sorry, I was just
saying hello, that's all."

"You can't come in here without permission."

"Well I didn't mean any harm, I just wanted to see
Sheamus," Gwen told him looking back at the steed.

"Those are the palace rules. If I find you in here
again, I'll have no choice but to report you to the

Prince and Queen," he threatened.

Gwen ignored the guard as she stroked Sheamus' neck "I'll see you again Sheamus, I promise."

Sheamus snorted and Gwen turned and walked out of the stables. The guard stood in the middle of the stable entrance with his arms crossed as he watched her go. A faint wind blew as she walked back to the castle. That feeling of being watched was back. She looked over her shoulder. There was nothing but two birds flying overhead.

Maybe I'm just having an off day, she thought.

That's when she noticed the gargoyles by the castle's gate were missing. She strolled around looking at the stone and touching the outside walls. Nothing happened. A closer look told her *all* the gargoyles were gone.

That's strange. Maybe this is a good thing. Maybe this means we're out of danger, she thought.

Gwen walked back inside. The uneasy feeling continued to follow her. As she walked down a hallway past a bust of the Queen, the head turned to look in her direction. Gwen quickly turned but the bust appeared as if it hadn't moved at all. The eyes were lifeless stone. A halfling walked by while smoking a pipe.

"I haven't seen you halflings a lot. What do you do during the day?" Gwen asked.

The creature removed the pipe from his mouth and held it in his furry hand, while blowing smoke rings.

"Well, we do lots of things. Some of us run the brewery and winery. Others take care of the study and all the books. Sometimes we help in the garden and, other times we go on adventures," the halfling said.

"I see, the castle is so big. I wonder why there isn't a village. There has to be more people living in the kingdom," Gwen said.

The halfling's eyes widened. He placed his pipe back in his mouth.

"Well, I must be going," he said, hurrying off towards the main hall.

"Wait, did I say something wrong?" Gwen asked.

"Perhaps someone can show you more of the castle. Have a lovely day!" he shouted.

Gwen, curious and confused at the same time, didn't understand what she said wrong. Why did so many beings, enough to make up a village, live in the castle. She walked around the staircase and saw a set of stairs leading down.

"I swear, this is the biggest castle I've ever seen," she said.

As Gwen walked down, two halflings walked up. Behind them she recognized the bard.

"Excuse me, I was wondering if someone could show me around?" Gwen asked.

"Sure, I have some time. What would you like to see?" the bard asked.

"A halfling mentioned a brewery, winery, and a study. I would really like to see everything. No one has really shown me anything," Gwen said.

"I would love to show you. I guess we met already. I remember you from dinner," she said with a friendly smile.

"Yes, you put on quite the performance." Gwen returned her smile.

"Thank you. I do love to entertain," the bard said as they walked to the bottom of the stairs. "So down here is the brewery and winery.

Phoebe led Gwen into the brewery. The ceiling was dark and curved, the stone walls covered with bricks. There were towering stacks of barrels against the walls.

"We make everything down here. Champagne, wine, beer, rum, you name it." Phoebe explained. "Down here we can control the temperature which helps with fermenting," she said.

As they walked around, halflings turned small knobs, filled kegs, and poured grains into malt mills. Harry and the ginger halfling with the braided beard clinked pints of beer.

"Cheers!" they shouted.

The halflings chugged the brew and wiped their faces heedless of the foam sloshed onto the floor.

"To sweet cream, Haggis," Harry pronounced.

"Tastes just like home, Harry," the halfling said, laughing gleefully.

"What is sweet cream beer?" Gwen asked.

"Oh! It's our own creation!" Haggis told her.

"It's liquid gold!" Harry shouted.

"Is it good?" Gwen asked.

"Is it good? It's just the most delicious beer in all the kingdom. You won't find this anywhere else blondie," Harry assured her.

"It's made with cream and sugar?" Gwen asked.

The two halflings looked at each other and burst into fits of laughter.

"It's our secret recipe. We don't share it with anyone," Haggis said, wiping tears from his big brown eyes.

"What other flavors do you make?" Gwen asked.

"There's a brew we created for the King called *Gold Whipped Beer*. It has gold flakes and tastes just like ice cream. We use different butters in our beers to give them a rich and savory flavor," a halfling with long brown hair with streaks of gray said.

"Wow, could I try it sometime?" Gwen asked.

"Well boys what do you say? Should we share our beer with the young maiden?" he asked.

"Give the lady a taste," a halfling across the way shouted.

The brown haired halfling held a glass in his hairy rough hand and poured the gold liquid from the keg before lifting the lid from a small wooden box and sprinkling some flakes into it and swirling it around.

Gold flakes glistened through the beer that the halfling handed to Gwen. They all turned to watch her. Gwen lifted it to her mouth and took a big gulp.

"Mmmm," she said as the smooth brew slid down her throat. She licked the foam from her top lip. "It's so rich and smooth. It's the best beer I've ever had."

All of the hin cheered.

"Thank you for sharing your magical potion with me," she said.

"Pleasure's all ours," Harry said.

"Would you like to see the winery now?" Phoebe asked.

"Oh yes, I would love to," Gwen said.

They walked out of the brewery and down the long tunnel past more barrels into a cellar. The walls were covered with shelves upon shelves of wine racks and bottles.

"Wow," Gwen whispered.

"This is where we store the wine, champagne, and all the other spirits," Phoebe said.

They left the wine cellar and approached an arched dark wooden door. The bard pushed the door open and golden sunlight spilled through the opening. Phoebe and Gwen stepped outside where row upon row of grapevines stretched all the way out to the wheat fields. Soft sunshine lit the horizon as the crystal blue sky transitioned into yellow and orange. A few halflings stomped grapes in the vats while wheat swayed in the distance. Gwen and Phoebe walked out into the vineyard. The plump grapes were mixed shades of purple.

"I can show you the study now if you'd like," the bard offered.

"Yes please. You know, the castle looks so big on the outside but seems even bigger on the inside. How many stories are there?" Gwen asked.

"It's currently ten stories but that can always change," Phoebe said as they walked back inside.

"What do you mean?" Gwen asked.

"Well, the castle grows sometimes, and we build extensions. It's full of secrets." The bard winked.

"What kind of secrets?" Gwen asked.

"There are many stories about the kingdom and this castle and its many rooms and hidden doors. You'll discover more the longer you're here," Phoebe explained.

"Maybe you could tell me some time," Gwen said.

"All will be revealed with time, dear Gwen," the bard replied.

They walked up a spiraling stone staircase to windows overlooking the vineyard.

"How high are we going?" Gwen asked.

They reached the top of the stairs, through an open doorway, and down a hall to a set of heavy cherry wooden doors. Phoebe pulled one open.

"After you," she insisted.

Gwen entered the grand library. It was long and wide with wooden arches that led to different sections. Exposed wooden beams curved horizontally over the ceiling. Lanterns hung all the way down to the end of the study. Upholstered antique furniture sat in different areas. There were desks, chairs, and a long cherry wood table. Walls made entirely of shelves were filled with thousands of books. The floor was polished and covered in burgundy paisley rugs. Portraits of the royal family in antique gold frames hung on the walls.

There was one of Prince Nicholas with his strong chiseled face, and one of the Queen in her crown. King Jericho appeared dressed in his crimson surcoat with beige fur collar and trim. A gold crown with rubies sat atop the King's head. The King and Prince shared the same chiseled appearance. Just beneath the hilt of the King's sword was a fiery dragon eye.

A hob stood at the top of a ladder, placing books on the shelves. Beyond him, Gwen found an arch that led into a tall cylinder-shaped room. It had a large dark chandelier that illuminated the coffered ceiling. In front of Gwen stood a large portrait of the King with the Prince as a little boy. King Jericho, with smiling eyes, stood behind Nicholas holding his shoulders. Nicholas appeared to be about ten years old.

Gwen moved on to stand before the same tall window Zilliah had looked through at the Prince. The brilliant blue sky dotted with cumulus clouds shimmered in golden rays through the window.

A sparrow chirped as it soared by flapping its wings. Gwen turned back and walked through the library where she saw two halflings sitting in chairs reading.

"Thank you for the tour, Phoebe. Is there anything else I should see?" Gwen asked.

"There's always more to see. I think you've seen all you need to for now. There are bedrooms, chambers, tunnels, allures, and ways around and about the castle," Phoebe explained.

"How do I get to the allure?" Gwen asked.

"It's on the top floor. You can take the same staircase we just climbed to get there. There are other staircases and passages as well. If you need anything, you know where to find me," Phoebe said.

"Thank you for everything Phoebe. It's nice to make a friend," Gwen said, smiling at the bard.

"Pleasure is all mine," Phoebe replied before she and Gwen went their separate ways.

Gwen went back to her room as day turned into evening. She sat on her bed pulling her hair over her shoulder when there was a knock on her door. She went to answer and saw Haggis standing in the doorway.

"Oh hello," Gwen greeted him.

"On behalf of myself and all the hin, we would like to present you with a gift," Haggis said, looking up at her with his hairy eyebrows.

"A gift? That's very kind of you. You didn't have to get me a gift." She looked down at the halfling's husky body.

"It's not for you," Haggis said, pulling a wooden tower into the doorway. "It's for the cat. We built this tree for the kitty."

The cat tree was almost as tall as the door. It was carved bark and wood. It had two small ladders, scratching posts, platforms, a small hammock, and a cubby for sleeping.

"We carved it out of an oak tree. We hope he likes it. The birds are stuffed with cat nip."

Gwen looked up at the crochet birds dangling from the branches. Snow jumped down from the bed and rubbed against Gwen's legs purring. Haggis offered the cat his hand. Snow sniffed him and allowed the halfling to pet him.

"Thank you and please thank all the hin for me as well. I'm sure Snow will love it," Gwen said.

She gave the halfling a smile and pulled on the tree. She grunted and pulled harder. She put her back into it, but the tree didn't budge.

"I'll put it in the room for you. Where do you want it?" the halfling asked.

"Next to the bookcase is fine, thank you," Gwen told him.

Haggis pushed the tree inside and next to the bookcase. Snow stretched to knead his paws on a post and jumped up onto a platform.

"Well look at that," Haggis said. The halfling smiled wrinkling his eyes.

"Thank you again. Have a goodnight." Gwen showed him the door.

Snow whacked a toy bird with his paw and ran up and down the tree, As he did, it magically grew nearly reaching the ceiling. More branches and green leaves appeared until it became a lush oak tree. Snow climbed all the way to the top.

Later that night, Snow slept inside the tree's cubby while Gwen slept in her bed in peaceful deep slumber.

Outside in the dark a soft wind blew, and something tapped the glass. It was a slow repetitive tap, faint and becoming louder. Gwen continued to sleep, but Snow looked up, one eye open. A moment later he lowered his head. He began drifting off when the tapping turned into nails clattering. The clattering then turned into screeching as the nails raked down the glass.

Gwen awoke and put her fingers in her ears. The balcony doors suddenly flew open, and the curtains flapped in the wind. Gwen quickly sat up and went to close the double doors. Outside the nightly winds still whistled. Gwen ignored them, crawled back into bed, and closed her eyes. She pulled the covers up around her head and fell back asleep.

A few moments later, the balcony doors flew open once more.

"You've got to be kidding me," Gwen whined.

She got out of bed again and closed the doors. Her sleepy eyes looked through the glass, but all she saw were twinkling stars in the night sky. She turned in the silence and found herself face to face with the crone.

Gwen's gasped at the sight of dark empty eyes staring into hers. The crone's jaws unhinged, her mouth dropped open, and a swarm of spiders scurried out. They ran across her cold gray face. The crone released a screeching scream as her long cold fingers closed around Gwen's throat. Her fingernails, yellow-gray, sharp like claws dug into Gwen's skin as she lifted Gwen off the ground. Gwen pulled on the crone's fingers and kicked her feet as the crone continued her piercing wails. Suddenly she released her grip, and Gwen fell to the floor coughing.

"Give me back my potion," the crone growled.

Her eyes never leaving the crone, Gwen crawled across the room pinning herself against the door. The crone twitched her wrist in the air and Gwen heard the door lock. She gripped the knob, and it burned her hand leaving a red blister. Gwen looked back at the crone whose eyes turned stone white.

Gwen rose and leaned against the wall. "I don't have your potion," she yelled.

"You dare lie to me?!" the crone asked, flying across the room towards Gwen. "I know it's here. Give it to me!" she shrieked.

"I told you; I don't have it!" Gwen shouted.

Spiders emerged from under the floorboards and swarmed towards Gwen.

"I'm only going to ask you one last time," the crone warned.

Spiders crawled from the ceiling at the corners of the room spreading quickly. Snow stood on top of his tree and growled at the crone. He gave an angry meow.

"I'll give it to you," Gwen cried.

The swarm of spiders stopped before Gwen's feet. The crone looked at Gwen with her eyes glowing and held out her hand.

Gwen charged at the crone. Spiders crawled up her legs as she ran. She charged, shoved the crone through balcony doors shattering the glass and sending her over the railing. Gwen nervously wiped the spiders off her arms and legs. As she did, they disappeared.

Gwen slowly stepped over the broken glass. The night wind blew faintly through her hair to the sound of waves on the shore. She paused at the rail and hesitant, she looked over the edge. From against the stone castle wall the crone looked up at Gwen. Her white eyes glowed as the crone snarled and scurried up the side of the castle.

Gwen stepped back and cut her foot on a shard of glass. She screamed as blood painted the broken glass. Running across the room with tears in her eyes, Gwen opened the door and fled into the castle. Snow ran out of the room after her.

Regaining the balcony, the crone's body transformed. Bones popped and cracked as she turned back into the black widow and leaped through the air. Spiders reappeared and scampered behind her.

Alerted by the commotion and drawing their swords, guards ran after the black widow. One man slipped in Gwen's blood and fell. Another of the guards slashed the black widow's side. She squealed in pain squirting blue blood. It didn't faze the crone; she continued limping along. Three guards gave chase with their swords at the ready.

Gwen looked back and stumbled over her own feet. The crone was quickly approaching her. Gwen scrambled to get up, ran around the corner, and down the hall. She swung the dungeon's door open and hurried down, her dress waving behind her. The prisoners yelled and screamed as Gwen fled past them to the far end and ducked behind a water barrel. In search of Gwen, the black widow jumped inside an open cell. Gwen quickly slammed the cell shut behind her. The spider hissed, fangs bared and gripped the bars with her shiny black legs. The crone's angry screech cause Gwen to jump back. She slipped in her blood and fell onto the dungeon floor.

Ripping off a piece of her dress, she wrapped it around her foot. The crone screeched again and spit venom. Gwen ducked and covered her head. The spider's poison splattered the cell walls. Yellow creamy liquid doused the guards who had just caught up to them. Gwen lifted her head and looked in the direction of the screams. The guards' skin was turning scarlet red.

"Ah! It burns!" a man cried, his muscles clenching. The others violently vomited.

"I can't breathe," one cried, his face turning from scarlet to violet.

More guards came running up. "What's going on?! What is that?!" a guard asked.

While he spoke, the crone transformed again, changing into an innocent little girl.

"What the..." another guard muttered.

They lowered their swords. The little girl wore a white dress with red hair tied in pigtails with pink bows. She had big blue eyes and dimpled rosy cheeks.

"Please, help me," she whimpered. "I just want to go home."

"Why is this little girl locked up?!" a guard asked as he approached her cell.

"No! Wait!" Gwen cried.

He stopped and turned to look at Gwen. When he did, the little girl's mouth opened wide. Spider's fangs glistened in her mouth. Her sharp tipped tongue elongated and swayed in the air. More blue eyes emerged on the surface of the little girl's face. She blinked all eight of her azure eyes as her slimy tongue wrapped around the guard's neck.

Yellow goo dripped onto his cheek burning his flesh. He grabbed at the crone's tongue as she squeezed tighter. The guard grunted, struggling to breathe. The crone pulled the guard closer. The back of his head hit the cell bars with a thud. His arms flailed and his face turned purple. Suddenly the guard's arms fell to his sides and his eyes closed.

Gwen snatched a sword from another guard and charged the cell. Lifting the sword above her head, she brought it down slicing off the crone's tongue. It fell to the floor, wiggled in a puddle of slobber, and disappeared in cloud of glittering purple smoke. The crone screamed, her mouth open wide like a black hole as her tongue regenerated. The little girl's innocent face returned.

"Good job Gwen. Keep her locked up and don't let her out," a guard said.

The men turned around and exited the dungeon.

"Please, I'm scared," the girl whimpered, rubbing her arms as tears filled her sparkly blue eyes.

"It's not going to work. You can't fool me. You're mine now," Gwen said, catching her breath.

The little girl flashed back into the crone. Her wrinkled pale hands grabbed the bars. "No!" she wailed. "I'll do anything! I'll give you anything you want."

"I don't want anything from you. I want you to rot," Gwen said.

"I can give you money, riches, jewels... a baby," the crone paused.

"A baby?" Gwen asked.

"Yes, isn't that what you've always wanted?" the crone asked.

Gwen looked at the crone's dark face and ghost white eyes.

"No, I won't do it. I don't need your magic," Gwen said turning to walk away.

"Wait!" the crone cried.

Gwen ignored her, left the dungeon, and slammed the door. Gwen walked past a table where a vase had spilled. Flowers lay spread out over the floor. She picked up the vase and placed the flowers back inside.

"It's okay Gwen. We'll get it cleaned up," a female's voice said.

Gwen looked down to see a brownie on the floor next to her foot.

"Thank you. I'm sorry for the mess," Gwen said.

"Go back to bed now, all will be clean by morning," she said.

Gwen went back to her destroyed room, curled up on the bed, and wrapped herself in a warm blanket. Snow leaped up to snuggle by her side. Outside the broken doors, the sun began to rise and the sound of waves on the shore lulled Gwen to sleep.

As she drifted in and out, Gwen peeked through her sleepy eyes. In the blur, the shattered glass began lifting itself off the floor. All the broken pieces hovered in the air and reassembled themselves, coming together like pieces of a puzzle. All the grooves, chips, and cracks in the glass slowly blended together. It was as if the glass was never broken.

Gwen's eyes opened wide. The sunlight shifted into a warm overlay of orange as she rose from her bed. The room was spotless. Snow slept curled inside the tree. Gwen walked over to pet him and kiss his head. He answered with a purr. Gwen yawned and looked down at her foot. The cloth was missing, her foot was healed.

Opening the bedroom door, she stepped outside. Snow jumped down from the tree, rushed with a meow, and followed her out of the room. They walked down the spiral staircase and out into the garden where they were greeted by the singing of morning birds. Snow walked by her side, looking up at Gwen with his bright blue eyes. She took a seat on a garden bench to watch the cabbage white butterflies flutter in the bushes. From the corner of her eye, she saw something shiny.

Gwen squinted and blinked before getting up and walking over. It was a gold handle laying on top of emerald leaves. She pulled it out of the shrub. It was a hand mirror with gold roses. Gwen brought it closer looking at her reflection. The mirror reflected a different expression than she knew was on her face. She blinked and shook her head. Gwen thought she was imagining the image when her reflection turned around showing the back of her head. The oval shaped mirror rippled like water. It calmed, sparkled in the sunlight and began showing her glimpses of things she had never seen before.

A gold key appeared. The top of it was shaped like a crown and decorated with diamonds and pink topaz. Gwen traced her fingers over the glass. The key slowly disappeared, replaced by an image of Nicholas smiling. Then, suddenly, her face reappeared. Gwen gasped and flipped the mirror over.

"Hey! Where did you get that?!" a hob asked.

"I found it. It was laying over there in the bushes," Gwen said.

"The mirror chose you? Hmm..." he muttered.

"Chose me? What do you mean?" she asked.

"That mirror belongs to the Queen. You best return it," he snickered, walking off into the garden.

Gwen looked at the back of the mirror with its gold roses and leaves. She hesitantly lifted it up and turned it back over. Nothing happened. The mirror appeared like any other ordinary mirror. Gwen walked through the garden when she noticed a postern. Snow followed her through it to the grand hallway and on into the main hall.

Gwen held the mirror hiding its reflection against her stomach as she walked nervously down the hall. Queen Helena spotted Gwen as she approached her.

"What do you have there?" the Queen asked.

"It's a mirror. I found it in the garden. One of the hobs told me it belongs to you," Gwen said.

"Oh dear! I lost that mirror decades ago before Nicholas was even born," the Queen said, her eyes wide.

"Well, I found it so now I can return it to you," Gwen said.

"Oh no, my dear. You don't understand," the Queen said.

"What do you mean? Don't you want it back?" Gwen asked.

"Even if I wanted it back, I couldn't. You see, the mirror appeared because it chose you," the Queen said.

"What do you mean it chose me?" Gwen asked.

"The mirror only appears when big changes are about to happen. It chose you, which means it has things to show you. That's not for anyone else. The mirror is an oracle. It will show you the future," Queen Helena said.

"That's why I saw things," Gwen said. "It was so... strange.,"

"You must be careful and handle it with great care. I have a box to go with it. You can keep the mirror safe in there. Wait here for a moment," the Queen said.

She lifted her gown as she left the hall. A moment later, the Queen re-entered carrying a pink metal box decorated with gold roses. She carefully lifted the lid and the sounds of a piano accompanied by chirping birds and wind chimes began playing. Gwen leaned closer and looked inside.

"The mirror is now yours to keep," the Queen said.

"Why is the box playing music?" Gwen asked.

"It is believed the oracle mirror was created by the muses. The music gives it its magic," the Queen said.

Gwen carefully placed the mirror inside the box. When she laid the mirror down, sparkling gold stars twinkled in its glass. They slowly floated towards the surface and spun out of the mirror. The stars arose above the box and Queen Helena slowly closed the lid.

"I must warn you, never leave the mirror exposed any longer than one hour. If you do, you will taint it and the mirror will become evil," the Queen said.

She placed the box in Gwen's hands as Snow purred and wagged his tail.

"If you ever taint the mirror Gwen, you must return it to the muses. The evil the mirror releases is unknown. Please follow these directions to protect everyone and ensure the safety of the kingdom," the Queen stressed.

"I will, I promise," Gwen said, looking into Helena's eyes.

"If you already looked into the mirror once, you must not do so again until that future is fulfilled. And do not look into the mirror more than three times. Choose what you wish to see wisely," the Queen said.

"Wish to see wisely? What do you mean?" Gwen asked.

"When you look into the mirror, ask it a question or tell it what you want to see. The mirror will answer you," the Queen said.

"It will answer me?" Gwen asked.

"Yes, it will show you in its reflection an answer to your question or request. This is no ordinary mirror. Don't look in it unless you wish to see the future," she said.

"Thank you, Your Highness.,"

She gave the Queen a curtsy, discreetly carrying the box hidden in her dress as she walked down toward the dungeon and the staircase that led up to her room. The crone saw her, wheezed deep, and hacked up phlegm from her throat.

"It's you," she squawked.

She had changed since being locked in the cell. The crone was now her true age. Her head was balding, and hunks of hair lay on the ground. Her wrinkled skin had started to rot. She slowly lifted her bony shaking hands and grabbed the cell bars.

"Look what you've done to me," the crone whimpered, a tooth falling from her grotesque mouth.

Her knees shook and her legs wobbled as she held tightly to the bars and looked at Gwen. A shade seemed to fall over the crone's white eyes turning them pitch black. Gwen gasped in fear and backed away. As she watched, the crone's body deteriorated and turned to ash. The daylight crept in through a tiny window falling on the gray ashes revealing specks of glitter. The crone was dead.

Gwen squatted down reaching her hand through the bars to touch the ashes. She rubbed her fingers together, sprinkled the dust, and smiled. She then stood up, turned around, and ran up the steps.

In the cell behind her an apparition of the crone rose from the pile of ashes. The crone's ghost hovered for a moment before slowly fading.

CHAPTER 8
LADY OF THE GARDEN

Gwen sat by the sea with her feet in the sand and the wind in her face, watching waves brush the shore. She took a deep breath of the briny air and looked up at the clouds drifting across the blue sky. Squawking seagulls soared over the waters. As the sun came out from behind the clouds, a salmon crashed through the surface of the sea and fell back in. Gwen inhaled again; the scents of guava, tangerine, and flowers filled the air.

Something shimmered under the water. Gwen stood up and walked closer, letting the waves wash over her feet. Her body swayed with the tides. Looking down, she saw pink, orange, and purple scales glimmer past her. The fish's iridescent tail broke through the waters and waved. When she held her hand over her brows to block the sun's glare, the creature disappeared into the sea. Suddenly, a woman's head with long blonde hair emerged from the sea, water dripping down her face and chin. Her cheekbones were accentuated with scaly gills. Her face was ethereal with shimmering turquoise eyes. Her shoulders and upper chest were human, but the tops of her breasts were covered with pink and gold scales. She wore pearls around her neck and a matching crown of shells on her head. A starfish squirmed in the hair on the side of her head. Translucent golden fins swirled and flared out from her hips.

When she blinked, her eyes transitioned from

turquoise to pink. Her long blonde locks flowed down
her arms and back. She rose until the sea swirled
about her waist. Her breasts were decorated with
pearls, seashells, and diamonds. A piece of net with
touches of diamonds and pearls flowed down her
stomach.

She began humming and singing, making Gwen
smile. The sweet sound seemed to ride across the
surface of the sea. The golden light of the sun
glimmered on the siren's jewels and scales. As Gwen
watched, the siren leaped into the air with a wave of
her tail and dove into the ocean.

The mermaid broke the surface as she swam to
some nearby rocks and lifted herself onto them. Two
more sirens appeared to join her. One had long wavy
blood orange hair and the other's was like black silk.
Their brightly colored tails shimmered with specks of
gold. The three sirens began singing. Entranced by the
song, Gwen walked along the shore toward them as
the song gradually grew louder and the sirens giggled
and smiled.

"Gwwweeennnnnn," the blonde siren sang.

When she reached them, Gwen didn't speak, still
caught up in the alluring melody. The dark-haired
siren fixed her gaze on Gwen. Strands of her black hair
waved on the wind and sun's light reflected on her
golden gills. Her honey eyes looked into Gwen's.

"Come Gwen," she sang, her voice soothing.

She waved her hands to the rhythm. While her
hands were delicate, her nails were sharp as claws. As
they sang a green cobra slithered from the rocks where
they sat. The siren flapped her fins. The three of them
looked down and released a high-pitched scream that
cracked the rocks where they sat. Then, the sirens
dove into the sea. The dark siren stopped a few feet
away and turned back to look at Gwen.

When she did, the other two sirens shot out of the
water and transformed into small birds. Their scales

became vibrant feathers. The sirens were smaller as roller birds, but their jeweled eyes sparkled just the same. The sirens song turned into sweet melodious tweets as they glided across the sea and disappeared over the horizon.

When they were gone, the cobra arose, lifted its head, hissed, and with a flash turned into the imp Bitzelsnick. Gwen didn't notice. She remained entranced gazing in the siren's direction. She made her way past the rocks standing high above the sea. Below the waves crashed down against boulders and sea stacks. Gwen stepped forward onto empty air and fell off the cliff heading for the boulders. White waters smacked the stone. Bitzelsnick snapped his fingers. Gwen's eyes widened.

"Ahhhhhhhhhhhhh!" Gwen screamed and reappeared on the solid ground of the cliff.

"Bitzelsnick," Gwen said.

"Hello deary," Bitzelsnick replied.

"Wait, I was just falling. How did I get back here?" Gwen asked.

Gwen furrowed her eyebrows. Bitzelsnick laughed.

"Oh, those sirens," the imp said, shaking his head.

"Where did you come from?" Gwen asked.

"I came to remind you of tonight's full moon Tonight, you must undo the hex on the prince and break the curse!" Bitzelsnick shouted.

"Oh, that's tonight?" Gwen asked.

"Yes, deary and you mustn't wait. Remember, you must give him the potion before the clock strikes midnight," he said.

"Yes, thank you Bitzelsnick. Thank you for everything," Gwen said.

"Don't thank me yet deary. I came to give you a warning."

"A warning? What about?" Gwen asked, furrowing her brows and shaking her head.

"I saw you capture the crone. Is she dead or did

she get away?"

"She's dead, why?" Gwen asked.

"Congratulations. You killed the crone. Now for the bad news," he said. The imp wiggled his foot in the rubble and looked down at the ground. "When she died, was there glitter in her ashes?"

"Yes, there was. It was so strange how it all happened."

Bitzelsnick heaved a heavy sigh.

"What is it? What's wrong?" Gwen asked.

"The crone isn't dead. And she can't die," he said.

"What? What do you mean?" Gwen shouted.

"Glitter in her ashes means the crone cast a spell before her death. The next girl that is born will be a reincarnation of the crone."

"Well, whose daughter will it be?"

"There's no way to tell. It could be anyone. But the next girl that's born will be the crone" he said.

"There has to be a way to stop her. To break her spell."

"The crone has an immortal soul. You must find a way to kill her so that she never reincarnates. If not, if you fail, I'll have no choice but to take the baby," Bitzelsnick said.

"Why would you take someone's baby?" Gwen asked.

"You must understand deary. You've seen her magic and evil ways. There are only two options. Either find a way to break her spell or, the girl must be destroyed," Bitzelsnick said.

"Can you help me break the spell?" Gwen asked.

"Oh no, deary. My magic is nothing compared to the crone's. As long as the crone lives, her evil will continue. You must find a way, or the baby will suffer a cruel fate. You're on your own with this one. Ta-ta for now deary." His eyes glowing citrine, his cheeks dimpled, and Bitzelsnick faded into dust and drifted off in the wind.

Gwen looked out at the sea with a heavy heart. She feared not only for the kingdom but for the life of someone's unborn baby. Gwen sat with her knees to her chest, her arms around her legs. Nearby, the waves crashed onto the rocks and seagulls squawked. Gwen hadn't seen anyone who was pregnant. As the sun started to set, she rose walked along the shore, the waves foaming over her feet.

She turned away from the shore. The breeze blew through her hair as she reached the grass and walked across a field. The sun set casting an orange glow against the darkening sky. She noticed the citrus and floral scents were gone replaced by those of saltwater and pine. Birds chirped and ruffled in the trees. The twilight turned to night as she reached the castle door and walked inside crossing the hall headed for the stairs.

"You're on time," Nicholas said. greeting Gwen with a smile. "Supper is soon if you're hungry."

"Wonderful, I'll go get washed up," she replied smiling coyly.

The Prince wore a white eye patch trimmed in gold that matched his royal attire. A scar went down the middle of his cheek and up through his brow. Gwen walked up the palace steps to her room and opened the door. Snow sleeping on top of the tree lifted his head and meowed. Gwen walked to the tree to pet him while he purred.

Leaving Snow, Gwen walked over to the nightstand and pulled the top drawer open. She grabbed the potion, held it in her hand, and smiled at the label, *Hex Breaker*. She closed her hand about it and left the room. In the dining hall, the guests were taking their seats. Gwen sat hiding the potion under her dress.

The gardener entered through a door from the grand hall and walked across the room to Gwen.

"Hello Madeleine," Gwen said.

The gardener was unimpressed. She gave Gwen a

sidelong glance and walked to the other side of the room. The Prince entered next and approached the table. He pulled a chair out and seated himself across from Gwen.

"Gwen how are you?" he asked, pulling at his jacket and looking up at her.

"I'm well Your Highness. Thank you. How are you feeling?"

"Feeling?" he asked.

"Yes, how are you doing since...well, you know," her voice faded away.

"I'm fine. It's just a paper cut," he said.

"I'm glad you're alright," she said with a shake of her head.

The Prince gave her an odd look as a hob placed a platter in front of him. Another hob placed one before Gwen and looked up at her.

"You're still here?" the hob asked looking down and spitting at Gwen's feet.

"That's enough Neville!" the Prince yelled.

The hob placed a crystal glass before the Prince, poured him a drink, snickered and shook his head.

"Leave us," the Prince ordered.

"Dinner smells lovely," Gwen commented.

"Excuse me for a moment," the Prince said.

He rose from his chair, placed his cloth napkin on the table, and exited the room. Gwen looked down the table. No one was paying attention to her. The hobs, gardener, knights, guards, halflings, Griswald, the butler, and the Queen all chatted among themselves.

Gwen took the potion from under her dress, slowly lifted the cork and the bottle popped open with a puff of gray smoke. A white skull appeared over the bottle. Gwen watched the image quickly dissipate before looking both ways down the table.

Suddenly, everyone froze as if time stood still. The Queen was holding a fork to her mouth. A guard held a glass before his mouth. Two hobs were frozen in a fit of laughter. Steam from the food hung in the air.

Gwen took the potion to where Prince Nicholas had sat before leaving the room. She put a single drop into his drink. The liquid rippled, fizzed and bubbled. Gwen added two more drops, and the liquid turned lime green.

"Oh no, Go down," Gwen shouted waving her hands at the green bubbles floating over the drink. When they popped, images of skulls appeared before the liquid turned into clear brown rum. She leaned forward, taking a closer look. The crone's eyes rose on the drink swaying side to side for a moment and dissolved. The potion in her hand turned to black smoke. Gwen gasped when time resumed, and chatter filled the room. After a moment, everyone reanimated. The Prince stood behind Gwen.

"Excuse me, may I take my seat?" the Prince asked.

"Oh yes, of course," Gwen said returning to her seat.

"Is something wrong?" he asked.

"Oh no, I just dropped my napkin," Gwen answered with a shake of her head.

She grinned and removed the lid from her bowl of steaming vegetable soup. She lifted a spoonful and gently blew on it. She watched as the Prince lifted his drink and drank every last drop. When he was finished, the Prince placed the glass firmly on the table, lowered his head to his chest and closed his eye.

"Nicholas?" Gwen asked. "Prince Nicholas? Are you alright?"

The Prince slowly looked up at Gwen and closed his eye again leaving her bewildered. His head remained motionless in his chest. Gwen reached across the table and shook the Prince's arm.

"Nicholas?" she shouted.

He grabbed her hand, his eye shot wide open, and his head perked up. He gave Gwen a malevolent stare.

She jumped out of her chair screaming. He released her and ripped off his eye patch off. The Prince's head began to shake and twitch. Everyone, except Gwen and the Queen, screamed and ran from the room.

"Nicholas," she muttered slowly rising.

Suddenly, the Queen's eyes widened in horror. The rapid movements blurred the Prince's face. His face transitioned between the cyclops and the prince over and over while his head twitched. Nicholas bellowed and it turned into a deep roar. The Prince rose from his chair, body shaking, arms dangling by his sides. His roars echoed across the castle. When the Prince's head stopped twitching, his true face was restored. Gwen released a sigh. Then, a second head emerged. The head of the cyclops grew from the Prince's shoulder.

For a moment the Prince was motionless. Then, the cyclops began wailing. Saliva drooled down his chin onto his jacket. His eye bulged in fury, canines protruded from his mouth. The cyclops looked up and bellowed anew shaking the ceiling. The Prince looked at the monstrosity on his shoulder as a whirlwind formed surrounding the Prince, Gwen, and the Queen. Flames from the chandeliers danced and the lighting in the dining hall flickered before being extinguished in puffs of smoke. The whirlwind stopped.

"Ahhh!" the Prince screamed.

Nicholas dropped to his knees and fell backward both heads hitting the marble floor. The cyclops' head turned into green smoke and faded away. The Prince's face was normal once more though he lay powerless and weak.

"Nicholas," Gwen cried.

The Queen rushed to her son's side. His face was white as snow.

"Nicholas!" the Queen shouted shaking the Prince by his shoulders.

His head tilted back, and his mouth dropped open.

His gums and tongue were gray.

"Nicholas," the Queen cried, weeping.

Gwen stood over the Prince, her eyes wide and quickly covered her mouth.

"You!" the Queen yelled her eyes drilling into Gwen. "What did you do to my son?"

"I...I didn't mean to," Gwen said.

The Prince gasped for air and his missing eye ripped through his skin. Nicholas blinked both eyes and opened them wide. Color returned to his cheeks and the Prince sat up.

"Oh Nicholas! You're okay!" the Queen shouted, wrapping her arms around his neck and holding him close.

"What happened?" the Prince asked.

"I don't know. But what matters is that you're okay," the Queen answered.

Nicholas slowly stood up and looked at Gwen.

"You...did you..." he paused.

Gwen's sad eyes turned to the Prince.

"Did you break my curse?" he asked.

Gwen took a deep breath and swallowed. "I think I did."

"But, how?" he asked. "And, why?"

"I stole the *Hex Breaker* potion from the crone because you were in pain," Gwen said.

The Queen stood next to the Prince and looked at Gwen. "You healed my son."

Helena stepped forward and embraced Gwen.

"And where's the crone now?" Nicholas asked.

"Dead, I hope," Gwen said.

"Dead? You killed her?" he asked.

"Yes, I believe I did. But I'm not sure."

The Prince turned and stormed out of the room.

"I'm sorry. I didn't mean to hurt anyone," Gwen cried.

"No," the Queen said, voice cracking and tears in her eyes. "You saved my son. I forgive you."

Gwen lifted her arms and embraced Helena. "I made a mistake."

Helena released her hold and looked at Gwen. "You did. But we all make mistakes. You saved my son's life. Thank you."

The Queen left leaving Gwen alone in the dining hall. Gwen went to her room where Snow slept curled on her bed. She walked out onto the balcony to look at the moon. It appeared bigger than she had ever seen it. The stars glittered in the navy-blue sky and pale moonlight glistened on the waters. Gwen watched the waves brush over the sand.

The clock struck twelve and the Prince didn't change. Nicholas sat on his bed and looked out his window at the moon. He slowly touched his face with both hands as tears filled his hazel eyes. A short time later, with a smile on his face, the Prince went to bed and so did the rest of the castle.

CHAPTER 9
THORNS & BRAMBLES

Everyone was sleeping except for Madeleine, the gardener. Madeleine stood at the kitchen sink washing dishes and looking out the window. She turned a crank, opening it and letting in a gentle gust of wind. Pale moonlight shined onto the kitchen floor. She carried plates to a cabinet and placed them on a shelf and returned to the sink. White, blue, and purple light faded in and out around the sink. Outside, glowing orbs hovered before the forest, floating around the trees.

Madeleine placed the plate on the counter keeping her eyes fixed on the orbs. She reached for them, but they were too far away. Tossing the dish rag over her shoulder, she walked out of the kitchen. As she passed through the swinging doors, the rag slipped off her shoulder and fell on the floor. Madeleine didn't seem to notice. Her gaze was fixed on the changing colors of the hovering orbs. The gardener following them, smiling as one floated before her face. She lifted a finger to touch it. The orb changed color and disappeared. When the orb reappeared, Madeleine pulled her hand away. The orb floated away into the forest and the gardener followed.

The further she went, the darker the woods became. Beneath the light of the blue super moon, the trees closed in on Madeleine. She followed the orbs to a clearing where they hovered, their glowing auras fading in and out. A fog rose from the ground and the orbs flew closer, circling her as they moved up and down. A wide smile spread across her face and her eyes sparkled. The gardener leaped, dancing through the mist, her eyes fixed on the orbs that began playing a song only she could hear.

Madeleine dipped and danced across the forest to the sound of violins and a piano. The music's pace picked up, and the gardener's dance followed the rhythm. The woods were quiet, and the air still. The only sound was Madeleine's feet sweeping through the grass. Madeleine took down her hair letting it sway as she danced. When she did, it took on streaks of gray.

The orbs began to whisper, their voices faint and fast. Madeleine suddenly gripped her ears, clenched her teeth, and her eyes teared. While the whispering orbs spoke, the gardener's skin grew wrinkled. Her hair changed to ghostly white. Age spots covered Madeleine's face; her eyes became dull. Still, Madeleine kept dancing to the music playing in her head.

The orbs glowed draining her life as the music slowly faded. The old woman continued dancing with her arms above her head, her frail frame wobbling in the moonlight. The music stopped playing and Madeleine stood at the edge of the forest. Her body swayed uneasily as the orbs encircled her. She held out her arms and looked down at her old, wrinkled skin and dangling white hair—and screamed.

Tears fell from her eyes as she watched the orbs change colors. At their bidding, she twisted her arms around her head and snapped her neck. Madeleine collapsed and the orbs floated down to her body before slowly disappearing.

The gardener's body quickly decomposed until all that remained was ivory bones. Her empty eye sockets looked up at the moon. Baby's breath, forget me not's, butterfly weeds, and yellow lantanas sprouted in Madeleine's rib cage, peeked from her nose, under her chin, and the top of her head.

***

In the castle, the morning sun greeted the cerulean sky. Gwen rose from her bed, placed her hand over her mouth, and yawned. Snow jumped down from his tree onto the bed and rubbed against Gwen. Outside her window, the birds chirped in their nests. Gwen changed into her mauve dress and left her room. Snow followed her down the stairs.

Nicholas spotted Gwen passing by from the corner of his eye and took a few steps back to look up at her.

"Good morning," he said, greeting Gwen with a warm smile.

"Uh, good morning," she said in the middle of a yawn

Gwen blinked, rubbed her eyes, and looked up into Nicholas's shining hazel eyes. The moment was broken by the shouting of hobs.

"Madeleine! She's missing," shouted a hob running through the main hall.

"What's going on?" the Prince asked.

"It's Madeleine. She's missing. No one's seen her all morning."

"Well, when did you last see her?" the Prince asked.

"Last night at dinner. Oh, Madeleine where are you?" the hob asked franticly.

"Calm down. We'll find her," the Prince assured him.

The hob settled down a bit and rushed into the kitchen. The window was open. He jumped up, pulled himself onto the counter and walked over to the window to crank it closed again. He jumped back down and ran out the double doors where he discovered the dish rag in the hallway. He kneeled to pick it up and saw the door was open.

"Hobs!" he shouted.

Four hobs ran to meet him in the hallway.

"What is it?" one asked.

"I know where Madeleine went," he said.

The hobs looked at the washcloth in his hand and the open door.

"Follow me," the goblin holding the rag said.

The hobs walked out the door and headed for the forest searching for footprints but found none.

"Madeleine!" a hob called.

They noticed the further they went; the more broken twigs were on the ground.

"This way," a hob said pushing through a bush with his clammy green hands.

The other goblins followed him until they found themselves in a clearing.

"Search the perimeters," the lead hob ordered.

The hobs scattered searching for the gardener.

"Ah, thorns and brambles," one shouted from the bushes.

Another hob brushed away the leaves, studying the ground.

"I found her!" a hob shouted in the distance.

The hobs rushed toward the sound of the shout. When they reached him, they saw the gardener's bones.

"It, it can't be...no!" one shouted.

"It is, it's her," another hob said in a low tone.

They looked at Madeleine. The forest had decorated her skeleton in its flowers.

"It's not her. This could be anyone," a hob said.

"How is it not her?" another hob asked.

"She's missing. The door was left wide open and here we are standing before a skeleton covered in flowers," he explained.

"Well," the hob muttered.

"That's what I thought. Now help me pick her up and let's take her inside. I don't want to hear anymore nonsense."

The hobs gathered around Madeleine.

"Be careful with her bones. On the count of three...one...two...three."

The goblins crouched down and lifted the skeleton. They walked through the forest carrying the gardener back into the castle garden and slowly lowered Madeleine onto a bench.

"How did this happen to you? What are we supposed to do now?" a hob sobbed.

"Cool it, Dave," another said.

"You found her," the Prince said, approaching the silent goblins. "How did this happen?"

"Are you saying we did this to Madeleine?" a hob asked.

"No, I'm asking how this happened," he answered.

"Well boys, it sounds to me like the Prince is blaming us," yet another hob said.

"I'm not blaming anyone. Does anyone know how this happened?" Nicholas asked again.

The hobs became infuriated. One by one they slowly stepped closer to the Prince.

"Hey, calm down. I'm just trying to help," Nicholas said.

The hobs snarled and growled. Their stumpy bodies shook as their green faces turned cherry red. Their pointy ears smoked. The goblins stopped shaking and their legs tightened, becoming thinner. Their bellies bulged, and their eyes glazed over turning black.

The hobs had turned into boggarts. They stormed into the greenhouse, scratching and clawing the soil splattering it on the ground. They smashed flowering pots, kicked over ferns, and trees, and dumped the water from the buckets. With a menacing cackle, one boggart turned on the hose and sprayed the birds. Another boggart lifted a wheelbarrow and flung it at the dome cracking the glass. They then ran into the kitchen, opened the pantry and dumped flour on the floor. The boggarts threw pots and pans across the room. One boggart climbed the counter and opened all the cabinets, smashing plates and teacups on the floor.

The Prince ran into the kitchen. "Stop it! Stop it now!" he shouted.

The boggarts ignored him and started throwing utensils. Flying forks spiraled through the air. The Prince dodged one that stuck in the door behind him. The boggart growled and sneered, grabbing knives. He gripped one in his fist and flung it at the prince.

Nicholas grabbed hold of the knife midair stopping it before it hit his chest. The blade slashed his palm.

"Enough!" he yelled.

The boggarts stopped. One held onto the knob of a cabinet while dangling in the air. He looked at Nicholas with his black eyes, growling and showing his sharp tiny teeth. All the boggarts turned their attention to the Prince.

"I'm sorry for what happened to Madeleine. I assure you it's no one's fault. I'm not blaming you. And I'm sorry," the Prince said.

The boggarts huffed and puffed angrily. One released a wooden spoon from his grip dropping it on the floor. The boggarts' bodies shook again, and they turned back into hobs.

"We will honor Madeleine. We will hold a ceremony for her. If you need to grieve then grieve. This was a tragedy that never should have happened. Madeleine will be dearly missed," the Prince said.

The hobs bowed their heads sad and ashamed. They walked past the Prince and left the kitchen. One goblin sniffled and wiped a tear from his eye.

The Prince wrapped his hand in a rag, applying pressure until the bleeding stopped. The hobs cleaned the greenhouse, sweeping up the spilled dirt and broken pots. The cracked glass on the dome repaired itself, blending seamlessly.

In the kitchen, they wiped down the counters and cabinets. They picked up broken ceramic pieces and placed them on the counter tops. The other broken pieces of ceramic rose from where they had fallen. Plates, bowls, and teacups reassembled themselves. All the kitchen cabinets opened themselves. Plates rose from the counters and stacked themselves inside the cabinet. The teacups flew across the kitchen landing inside a cabinet. Drawers slowly slid open. Spoons, forks, butter knives, whisks, ladles, measuring spoons, and spatulas floated across the kitchen into the drawers.

The spilled honey refilled the jar. Two hobs lifted a sheet of glass while another stood outside. They pushed the glass up and it flashed into place. The hob cranked the window closing it. A halfling entered the kitchen through the door carrying a bag of flour. He opened the pantry and placed it on a shelf.

CHAPTER 10
IN BLOOM

The next morning, Snow followed Gwen as she wandered out the gate toward a pond and the forest beyond. She was worried about the unborn baby. A gaggle of geese wobbled by, flapped their wings and honked, but Gwen kept walking. She stopped for a moment to look around and spotted a blue wisteria, the wind ruffling through its flowers. She picked Snow up and carried him past the flowering tree.

She came upon a waterfall, put the cat down, and sat by the water listening to the falling waters and rustling leaves. As she meditated, pink rose buds appeared in the grass. Gwen began radiating soft light and levitated. While Gwen hovered in the air, yellow orchids, lilies of the valley, and pink daisies with green centers blossomed around her.

Gwen found she was suddenly naked. Her hair flowed over her breasts as she sat in the air with her legs crossed and her arms draped over her knees. A daisy bloomed in Gwen's hair. Birds whistled and chirped. Gwen smiled and her jade irises sparkled with gold. The forest floor was covered in lush pink roses. The roses lifted off the ground, hovered, and turned into pink butterflies that came together forming the silhouette of a woman.

The wind picked up and swirled around her, and Gwen slowly drifted to the ground. The silhouette changed into the maiden, Sinnafain. She approached to look into Gwen's eyes, smiled and tilted her head.

"You're ready," she whispered.

"Ready for what?" Gwen asked.

"To step into your power. Your destiny awaits," she said.

"My power? I'm just a human. What destiny?" Gwen asked.

The maiden slowly backed away and metal began to cover Gwen's body. Her feet were encased in shining platinum boots that spread up her legs. Plates covered her knees as the metal continued up her thighs. It wrapped around her hourglass waist and spread across her chest. Reflective pauldrons covered Gwen's shoulders. Platinum spread down Gwen's arms covering her elbows and hands. When Sinnafain lifted her head, Gwen stood before her, a warrior. The gold faded from Gwen's eyes.

"What's this for?" Gwen asked.

"Protection. You're going to need it," Sinnafain said.

"Need it for what?" Gwen asked.

"You'll see. Your life is just beginning," the maiden told her.

Gwen looked at Sinnafain puzzled. The maiden smiled and became a flock of pink butterflies that fluttered away.

"Wait! What do you mean my life is just beginning? I'm forty years old! And what about my dress?" Gwen shouted.

There was no answer. Gwen furrowed her brows and looked down at her armor. She touched the plate on her stomach.

"Warrior," she whispered.

She recalled the mirror and remembered the reflection showing her the Prince smiling and her eyes beaming like lasers.

"The mirror," she uttered under her breath. "The mirror. Maybe the mirror can show me how to break the crone's spell."

She walked back toward the waterfall and Snow ran after her.

"I can't go back to the castle like this. They'll want to know where I got the armor. They'll think I stole it," Gwen said.

Snow ran up behind Gwen, meowed and walked in front of Gwen sniffing her.

"It sure is something, isn't it?" she asked.

Gwen stopped walking and she started testing her armor. She lifted her leg and kicked the air. Metal clunked and she fell to the ground.

"Ah! That's heavy," Gwen said.

She stood back up and moved her arms around. Gwen pushed one arm out in front of her. A shield appeared in her hand. She drew her arm back and stood up straight. Her hand hit something on her waist. She looked down and saw a handle. She gripped it and pulled out a long sword and slid it back into the scabbard. The forest filled with whispers and giggling.

Gwen looked around but didn't see anything. The laughing stopped when Gwen continued walking. A moment later, she heard it again. She stopped and the forest grew quiet.

"Ow!" Gwen shouted as something electric jolted her shoulder.

"Ow! Ow! Ow!" she shouted, her arms, hands, stomach, legs, and feet receiving shocks.

She lifted her foot and hopped around, swiped and slapped where she saw a spark. Gwen kept getting shocked. As she ran through the forest, she shook her head and brushed her hands through her hair. The shocks stopped. Embers twinkled in the air.

"Get away from me!" she shouted.

The creatures giggled and faded into focus. Gwen was surrounded by sprites.

"What do you want? Leave me alone," she shouted at them.

The tiny creatures fluttered on translucent

butterfly wings. They were small like fairies but had silvery blue skin. Their eyes were large and gold. They had tiny noses, small mouths, and heart shaped faces. Their ears peeked out through their hair. The females wore tiny dresses and had long hair. The males wore pants with short sleeved shirts and had short hair. None of them wore shoes.

"What are you doing in our forest?" a sprite asked in a high pitch feminine voice.

"Your forest? This is the kingdom," Gwen said.

"No. This is our forest and you're trespassing," the sprite countered in a voice that was whiny and shrill.

"Well, I was leaving until you started shocking me," Gwen said.

The creatures giggled again. Gwen looked around and saw eight sprites. The creatures' skin and eyes glowed in the shade.

"Say, how about a trade?" a sprite asked. The sprite wore a dress with long flowing hair, but its voice was deep.

"A trade? I'm not giving you anything," Gwen said walking away.

When she did, the sprites attacked her again. The sprite in the dress flew buzzing her wings and shocked Gwen's buttocks. The sparks glittered in silver and white. The sprites swarmed around Gwen giggling. Another sprite flew after Snow and shocked his tail. A second sprite shocked the cat's paw. Snow's ears drew back. He raised his paw and hissed.

"I'm warning you. Back off," Gwen shouted.

They continued giggling and shocking Gwen. Her armor sparked on her back and calves. Gwen drew her sword. The handle sprouted vines and wrapped around her arm. The vines spread all the way up her shoulder and bloomed with water lilies. The blade turned iridescent and flared at the tip. Gwen gripped the weapon with both hands. The sprites giggled. Gwen swung hitting a sprite. The blade sparked shocking the creature. It flew and hit a tree.

All the sprites gasped when Gwen drew back and swung again. The sprites sparked and flew across the forest. Gwen lifted the sword above her head clenching her jaw and waved the blade in the air. The sprites' skin turned white where the blade touched them. A sprite in a dress soared charging through the air. It struck Gwen's face, shocking her cheek.

Gwen smacked the sprite to the ground. The creature lay on its back looking up at Gwen holding her sword pointed at the sprite's throat.

"Leave me alone," Gwen demanded.

The sprite's eyes widened, and it vanished. Snow clawed the air reaching for a sprite wearing pants. It blinked out. The cat pounced toward a sprite in a dress.

"I'm out of here!" the sprite shouted.

Gwen panted and put her sword away. She tucked her hair behind her ear and walked out of the forest.

CHAPTER 11
THE BLUEBIRDS BALLAD

Gwen and Snow entered the main hall of the castle and heard strange noises coming from the crowded room. A crowd had gathered there, and whispers filled the room.

"Did you hear about the gardener?" one halfling asked another.

"No. What happened to Madeleine?" the halfling asked.

Gwen walked through the crowd making her way to the middle of the room where she saw Phoebe.

"What's going on?" Gwen asked.

"Oh Gwen, it's such a tragedy. A shame really," the bard wept.

Phoebe wiped tears from her eyes as Gwen looked up to see the Queen on a landing overlooking the room. Helena, in her gold ballgown and crown glanced down at everyone, and the chatter ceased.

"Thank you all for coming. Today is a sad day. We are gathered together to mourn the loss of Madeleine who passed away last night," the Queen said.

Gwen gasped. "What?" Madeleine died?" she whispered to the still crying Phoebe.

"Today we honor Madeleine and her hard work as gardener and keeper of the greenhouse. If you'll please join us in the greenhouse, the hin has arranged a memorial for our beloved gardener," the Queen said, turning and walking away.

Loud chatter filled the room. Everyone walked out

and down the grand hall.

"I wonder what it is," Thomas said looking up at his father as everyone walked under the mural of heaven and cherubs to the greenhouse.

Hobs stood on either side of the entrance and walked in behind the group. Gwen looked up to see the top of an oak tree that nearly reached the glass ceiling. Bluebirds sang while they flitted about the tree's thick branches. Gathering in the middle of the greenhouse, the group stood before a platform where an ivory tarp covered a tall figure.

"Everyone gather around," the Queen instructed.

The chatter quieted as everyone directed their attention to the Queen.

"The hin would like to present you all with a very special gift," the Queen said, waving her arm. "Phoebe, if you will."

The bard stepped forward pushing aside a hob as she made her way out of the crowd to the platform. The bard walked up the steps and stood before the covered figure before turning to face the crowd.

"Hello everyone, thank you all for coming." The bard sniffled and wiped her nose. "Excuse me, I'm sorry. I asked you all here today on behalf of myself and the hin as we remember Madeleine, our beloved gardener. The hin and I wanted to make something special to honor Madeleine and keep her memory alive in our hearts."

She gripped the tarp pulling it off unveiling a statue of Madeleine in her overalls.

Her hair was braided in pigtails. A stone bird sat in the palm of her hand as she looked up and smiled.

"I present to you the Madeleine memorial," the bard shouted.

"It's so beautiful," a hob said, tearing up and wiping the corner of his eye.

"It sure is," another said, wrapping his arm around the first's shoulder.

Phoebe stepped down from the platform, and balls of light floated from the statue. The crowd gasped as the orbs drifted through the crowd. A ball of light hovered before Haggis's face transitioning from white to blue to purple. The halflings eyes widened and his mouth spread into a wide smile. As if in a trance, all the other beings started smiling as well.

"What the..." Gwen muttered. "Harry?"

She waved her hand in front of his face. The halfling didn't blink. More orbs floated from the statue filling the room. Gwen spotted the Prince standing before the door. Nicholas had a smile on his face. Gwen walked over to him. She waved her hand in front of the Prince's face.

"Nicholas?"

Everyone in the room began to sway and dance while storm clouds darkened the sky. Thunder cracked and rain poured down. Hobs joined hands, guards, knights, and the hin swayed back and forth dancing a waltz to the music playing in their minds. All Gwen could hear was the sounds of rain tapping the glass and feet stepping on the floor.

The gardener's statue sprouted flowers and bloomed. Tiny buds emerged from her stone head, down her neck, to her legs and opened into small petals. A small crack appeared on the statue's head and continued to spread past the gardener's eye to her chin. Some of the stone crumbled to the floor revealing the gardener's skeleton was inside.

Gwen quickly looked away from the orbs and noticed Snow was missing.

"Snow!" she shouted, her voice echoing across the greenhouse.

Gwen walked through the crowd and stood on tiptoe looking for the cat. An orb appeared before her and hovered near her face. Music started to play in her head. Gwen turned and ran to the door. Outside, the sky grew darker, thunder roared, and rain crashed against the glass in a downpour.

The orbs glowed brighter, flew around faces and danced in the reflection of their eyes. Gwen opened the door and ran out of the greenhouse where she spotted Snow. She picked him up and looked back over her shoulder. Everyone in the room was dancing, but she noticed the hobs were aging. Phoebe's eyes darkened and the hobs' green skin wrinkled. She opened another door and ran outside into the garden, her boots splashing in the puddles.

"Leux!" Gwen shouted, looking up at the storm with raindrops streaming down her face. "Leux!"

She waited, but nothing happened. Through the greenhouse glass, she saw Queen Helena's head. Her crown was askew as she swayed from side to side. Thunder cracked and lightning flashed illuminating the Queen's face. She had turned into an old, withered, decrepit woman with ashy skin. Her cheeks drooped, her eyes were sunken, and her lips were gray. Helena wore a ghoulish grin.

Lightning flashed and thunder rumbled as Gwen ran through the garden and back inside the greenhouse. The Prince's hair had turned dark gray. She covered her eyes, averted her gaze, and pushed through the crowd. Gwen ran up to the platform and waved her arm. The iridescent shield materialized in her hand, shimmered, and sprouted vines and water lilies.

"No, no, no! I don't need a shield! I need something else!" she shouted.

Gwen shook her arm, and the shield fell to the floor. A crack zig zagged across the greenhouse. Concrete and dirt flew out of the ground in waves. All the dancers levitated into the air while the floor repaired itself. A ginormous shimmering field of blue and purple rose from the ground. A translucent veil closed around everyone, and the creatures stopped dancing. One by one, old and weak, they fell helplessly to the floor.

When Gwen stood up, Leux's glistening golden scales glided around the dome behind her. The dragon grumbled and the storm clouds disappeared. The birds began to chirp and flew across the greenhouse. The door flew open, and the wind blew in as Leux the wizard appeared in the doorway with his staff in hand.

"Hello Gwen," he said stepping over bodies as he walked her way.

"Leux, you came," Gwen said.

"What happened here?" he asked looking around.

"I don't know. There were these glowing orbs," Gwen said.

"Ah yes. Whispering wisps. Nasty little buggers."

"Everyone was smiling and dancing," Gwen added.

"Stand back," Leux instructed.

The wizard slammed his staff on the floor. The force field shimmered. An orb flew at Leux's face. The wizard swung his staff, and the orb disappeared into the gemstone. More orbs flew toward the wizard. One by one they flashed into the stone. Leux switched hands and moved his staff sideways. A white light flashed inside the staff's topaz. The wizard pursed his lips and wiggled his mustache and his body shook. Leux steadied his footing. The wizard closed his eyes, lifted his staff, and slammed it on the ground again. All those on the floor glowed white. The wind picked up and blew away their aging. One by one, they sat up.

"Thank you," Gwen said.

Leux opened his eyes which flashed with a bright cerulean blue light.

"Helena!" Gwen shouted, retracting her shield and rushing to the Queen's side to help her up.

"What happened?" Helena asked.

"Orb creatures called whispering wisps took Madeleine. You're going to be okay," Gwen said.

Restored, everyone stood and followed the Queen

out of the greenhouse.

Gwen reached down and picked Snow up as they left the dome. She placed Snow on the marble floor outside, turned the corner and headed up the spiral staircase back to their room.

Snow jumped up on the bed and licked his paws while Gwen walked over to the box with the hand mirror. She lifted the top and took the mirror out.

"Can you show me how to break the crone's spell?" Gwen asked.

Her reflection swirled in the mirror. It stopped when Gwen looked at a ship out at sea.

"The sea?" she asked.

The image within became a weeping willow and a book sitting in the grass under the tree. That image faded and a skeleton key appeared.

"Why do I keep seeing this key? Where is it and what do I do with it?" Gwen asked.

The gold key faded away and Gwen was looking at her reflection. She saw herself in her armor for the first time. She placed the mirror back in the box, covered it with the lid, and placed it inside the drawer. Gwen ran out of the room and rushed down the steps.

"Griswald!" Gwen called, spotting him on the other side of the room. "Griswald, I need a favor."

"What can I do you for Gwen?"

"I need a ship."

"A ship? Why do you need a ship?" he asked.

"The crone. I captured her in the dungeon, and she died. But not really. She cast a spell before her death. She will come back reincarnated as the next girl born. I must stop her," Gwen said.

"A ship it is then," Griswald said with a nod of his head.

"Griswald, you're the best. Thank you so much," Gwen said, following him across the hall.

"I assume you won't be traveling alone," he said.

"I won't?" Gwen asked.

"Well, no it's too dangerous. Surely someone's told you the tale of *The Fishermen Sea?*" Griswald asked.

"No, I haven't heard anything," Gwen said.

"You come to me asking for a ship and you're oblivious to the danger that awaits you? Someone must accompany you on this venture." Griswald replied.

Gwen paused for a moment then lifted her finger.

"The hin! Yes, the hin will be joining me," she said.

"If it wasn't because of the crone, I wouldn't be helping you," Griswald said, sighing and rolling his eyes.

The dining halls doors swung open, and the Prince walked in.

"What's this? Did I hear *The Fishermen Sea* being bandied about?" he asked. His voice was deep and stern.

"The girl wants a ship," Griswald said.

"A ship? Absolutely not," the Prince said.

"And why not?" Gwen asked.

"Why not? It's too dangerous!" the Prince shouted.

"I won't be traveling alone. I'll have the hin with me," Gwen said.

"Absolutely not! I forbid it!" the Prince shouted.

"Forbid it? You can't forbid me. Who are you to tell me what I can and cannot do?" Gwen asked.

"I am the Prince. I am in charge of this kingdom, and yes Gwen, I forbid it. You and the hin will get yourselves killed."

"Well, I'm going, and you can't stop me," Gwen countered.

"Don't you understand?! Men have died sailing those seas. It earned its name for a reason."

"I won't die," Gwen said shaking her head at the Prince.

"How do you know that? You don't know what creatures lurk deep below the sea's surface. I'm not trying to be a jerk. I'm sorry if I need to be, but my job is to keep you safe," the Prince said.

Gwen crossed her arms and sighed. "Since when? I go outside and travel the kingdom all the time. I walked the *Wheat Fields*. I passed *The Dragon Lands*, I've been to the mountains, and I went to the crone. Where were you?" she asked.

"Where was I? I found you in the woods after you almost died from that giant earthworm. When you released Zilliah, I went and killed her before she could kill anyone else. The crone could have killed you. You're lucky she didn't. Where was I? Here, watching over the palace, repairing the dungeon, and keeping everyone safe. If something were to happen to you Gwen, I don't know what I would do."

"I was just fine after that worm. I didn't need your help. I defeated the crone by myself. I'm the one who broke your curse. I don't need you to save me. I can fight my own battles," Gwen said.

"You can't do everything yourself Gwen. You're not invincible. You're human. If you don't want to listen to me—fine. I've said what I have to say. I don't want to lose you or the hin," the Prince said.

"Then I'll go alone. The hin can stay here. I'll be okay," Gwen said.

"No Gwen, you will not be okay! I'm telling you not to go. Will you please just trust me?" he asked.

"Nicholas, this isn't about trust. The crone can be reincarnated. I'm going, and you can't stop me."

"Griswald, if she goes then make sure she doesn't travel alone," he said.

"Yes, your majesty," Griswald said.

"You can't control me. An unborn baby's life is at risk. If the crone reincarnates then all the lives in the kingdom are at risk."

"I can't control you. You've been free to go whenever you want. You're right, who am I to stop you," he said and walked away.

"The ship will be waiting for you in the morning. Be

sure the hin are ready to go," Griswald said.

"Thank you. I'm glad someone around here understands," Gwen said.

Griswald turned without a word and left the room. Gwen sighed. Suddenly alone, she went in search of the hin.

She came upon Phoebe, the halfling, standing outside the greenhouse talking to a hob.

"I just thought if you need anything, I could help you harvest. Or maybe help with the garden," Phoebe said.

"We don't need your help! Go back to playing your flute and being a bard!" Neville said.

"I could do both," she said.

"Your job is to play music and entertain. We don't need you bothering us. We have the garden and greenhouse under control. Now beat it." He slammed the door rattling the glass.

Gwen went to Phoebe. "Are you okay Phoebe?" she asked.

"Oh, hi Gwen. Yes, I'm fine. I just wanted to be nice and help in the garden," she said.

"I know Phoebe. Don't let those hobs get to you. Their bitter little creatures," Gwen said.

Phoebe laughed and snorted. "You're right. What can I do you for?"

"I want to ask you for a favor," Gwen said.

"Of course, Gwen. What do you need?" Phoebe asked, looking up at Gwen with her big brown eyes.

"Well, would you be willing to travel with me on a ship across the sea?"

"Oh Gwen. I know I said anything, but I don't know about that," Phoebe said.

"It's important," Gwen said and explained about the crone's spell.

"Oh, that's awful. I'll do it but only for the baby," she said.

"Thank you, Phoebe. I knew you'd understand,"

"We'll have to find hin to join us. Come with me."

Phoebe led Gwen down the grand hallway. Together they walked up the stairs, past the study, and higher up in the castle than Gwen had ever gone before. They walked down a hallway passed a mirror with a wooden frame.

The mirror came to life. Menacing waves crashing on the shoreline. Water poured out of the frame and streamed down the wall. The crone appeared in the storm, her body and face made of water. She lifted herself out of the frame and reached for Gwen with her claws.

"Phoebe!" Gwen screamed.

The crone strangled Gwen, digging her claws into her skin and trying to pull her into the mirror.

"Gwen!" the halfling shouted.

Gwen grabbed hold of the crone's hands and tried pulling them from her neck while gasping for air. Sharp claws pierced Gwen's skin, and she started to bleed.

"Take my hand!" the halfling shouted, reaching for Gwen.

Metal amour covered Gwen's hands. The metal turned orange and then red, burning the crone. She released her hold. Gwen stumbled forward coughing. When she turned to look at the mirror, the crone was gone. The frame swung on the wall and fell to the floor.

"Are you alright?" Phoebe asked.

"Yeah, I'm fine," Gwen said.

Gwen slowly lowered her hands revealing bruises on her throat.

"You'll be okay. Come, this way," Phoebe said.

Gwen and Phoebe walked down the hall. They stopped before a door.

"He'll help us," Phoebe said, opening the door.

"Phoebe. What brings you here?" asked a male halfling wearing a white shirt, suspenders, and brown trousers.

He took the pipe from his mouth and held it in his hand.

"This is my friend Gwen," Phoebe said.

"I've seen you around. Please, come in."

The cherry wood door was shorter than all the other doors in the castle. Gwen slouched down and walked through. When she stood up, she was as tall as the ceiling.

"Thank you for inviting us in. It's quite...cozy," Gwen said.

"Our small rooms remind us of home," the halfling said with a warm smile.

He walked across the floor and sat down in a rocking chair next to a small window to smoke his pipe.

"Pleasure's all mine. Make yourselves at home," he said.

Gwen sat cross legged on the floor. On the wall next to her was a painting of a clipper ship sailing the seas. While she looked at the picture, the ship rocked upon the waves and a gentle breeze blew on Gwen's face.

"What brings you by?" the halfling asked.

"We need a favor. And I couldn't think of a better man for the job," Phoebe said.

"Certainly, what can I do you for?"

"Have you heard of the crone?" Gwen asked.

"Oh yes. I've heard many stories," he replied, his smile turning to a frown.

"Well, we're looking to sail the seas. But I can't go alone," Gwen told him.

"The sea." The halfling leaned forward in his chair.

"Yes, the sea. I need to find the crone's spell book. It's the only way to break her curse."

"Dear girl, do you know what that will entail?" he asked.

"I'm ready for whatever comes our way. A baby's life is at risk and so is the entire kingdom," Gwen said.

"And where do you suppose we will find this spell book?"

"I'm not sure. An oracle showed me the sea and then a weeping willow."

"With all due respect miss, you're in over your head," he said.

"Maybe, but it wouldn't be fair to the life of an unborn baby to never live her true purpose. Her soul would be taken away and replaced with the crone's. And the crone would continue wreaking havoc on the land."

"Have you discussed this with the Prince?" the halfling asked.

"I have," Gwen said.

"What did the Prince say? Surely, he doesn't support this journey."

"Never mind what the Prince said! I will go and break the crone's spell with you or without you," Gwen informed him.

"Well, we can't have a baby come into this world as a reincarnation of the crone. The journey won't be easy. Luckily for you, I know these seas well. We shall gather the hin and set sail in the morning."

He blew smoke rings above his head and stood.

"I have what we need," he said walking across the room to a shelf.

He searched through the books, tilted one, and pulled out a folded piece of paper. He walked back to the table where he opened the map.

"This is a map of *The Fishermen Sea*," he said picking a taper out of the candle holder.

The wax dripped on his hand as he held the candle over the map. In the soft light, writing in silver ink appeared through the parchment. In the corner was an image of a compass. In the top right appeared *Sir Jericho's Kingdom*. The upper left was labeled, *The Dragon Lands*. Beside that were mountain peaks. The remainder of left side showed *The Fishermen Sea*.

Beside the sea was an outline of the castle. The halfling moved the candle over the hills by *The Wetlands* and the ink turned from silver to green.

"There's your weeping willow and spell book," the halfling announced.

He held the glowing candle closer to his face and the map's ink seeped back into the paper. He placed the candle on the table and looked at Gwen over his glasses.

"The sea certainly seems to be our best route. I'll see you in the morning, bright and early. Don't be late."

"Oh, thank you, Fitz. Thank you for everything," Phoebe said.

"You're welcome. Now, go get some rest. A big day lies ahead."

Gwen rose and hit her head on an iron chandelier. "Ow!"

Fitz smiled as he walked Gwen and Phoebe to the door. Fitz slowly closed the door behind them. When he did, the door vanished into the wall.

"Where did the door go?" she asked.

"The hin like their privacy," Phoebe said.

"How strange."

"I told you, the castle is full of secrets," the bard said and laughed.

"I guess so," Gwen muttered.

She and Phoebe walked down the hall. Gwen noticed she wasn't moving. Her legs were moving but she seemed to be walking in place as the floor shifted underneath her.

"What's going on?" she asked.

"Stand still, you'll see," the bard told her.

The railing began moving and Gwen grabbed hold of the wood. She looked up and saw the upper levels turning counterclockwise. She looked down to see the same thing happening below. The speed of the floors picked up and Gwen held on tighter. Phoebe stood in the middle of the hall laughing. The railings finally slowed and locked into place.

"What just happened?" Gwen asked, letting go of the railing.

"New floors and rooms were added. It happens sometimes," Phoebe said.

"But why? Isn't the castle big enough already?"

"Depends. Sometimes new guests come to stay. Other times another room is needed for something. Maybe the library was expanded or maybe they moved the ballroom," Phoebe said.

"There's a ballroom?" Gwen asked.

"Yes of course there's a ballroom. The castle has every room you can think of," Phoebe said.

"That's interesting. I haven't seen the ballroom."

"It's only used for parties and special occasions. It's downstairs past the throne room. I better turn in. The sun is setting. Have a goodnight, Gwen."

A door appeared in the wall. Phoebe turned the knob, walked inside, and closed it behind her leaving Gwen alone.

CHAPTER 12
ELIXIR KISS

After Phobe disappeared, Gwen continued down the hall and around the square staircase where she spotted Prince Nicholas.

"Gwen," he greeted her.

She turned to look at him. "Yes?"

"If you go, be safe. I don't want anything to happen to you."

"Of course, Your Highness. I understand," Gwen said.

"Good. When I was a boy, men sailed *The Fishermen Sea* to bring us food and other goods. The waters are difficult during storms and many monsters live below the surface."

"What kind of monsters?" Gwen asked.

"Once a group of men were lured in by sirens. They sang their sweet song enticing them. Their beauty was hard to resist and put them in a trance. The men tied up the ship and joined the sirens on the rocks. The creatures sucked the souls from their bodies and devoured the men, crunching on their bones. But sirens are just one of many creatures living out at sea. Men have been lost at sea and never seen again."

"Sirens, do they harm women or just men?" she asked.

"Why? Have you seen them?"

"I'm just wondering," Gwen answered.

"I don't know. Women have never sailed the seas. But it doesn't matter, there are still many other dangers for men and women," he countered.

"I understand. I know you care about me and the kingdom. I respect your position as Prince. But I'm a grown woman. I can take care of myself. Thank you for the warning but I'm going," Gwen said, looking into Nicholas's hazel eyes.

"I don't want to see you get hurt, Gwen," he whispered to her.

She looked down for a moment and then back at Nicholas.

"My job is to protect everyone in the kingdom. I won't stop you. I trust you'll do what is right."

"Okay," she said still looking into his eyes.

"I never thanked you," he said.

"For what?"

"For breaking my curse. I don't know why you did it. You put yourself in danger to help me. You didn't have to," he told her.

"You were unhappy and in pain. I've never met anyone like you Nicholas. You're kind. No matter what happens. I just want you to be happy," Gwen said.

The Prince stepped closer. Gwen could hear herself breathing. Nicholas leaned in and his lips met hers. Gwen wrapped her hands around his head and ran her fingers through his hair. He drew her closer, placing his hands on her hips and smiled through their kiss. Gwen sighed, tasting his elixir kiss.

He pulled away still smiling as they both breathed heavily. All of Gwen's senses were tingling as she stared into Nicholas's glimmering eyes.

"Goodnight Gwen," he whispered.

Nicholas turned and walked away while she watched his every step. When he reached the end of the hall, he turned to look back. Gwen helplessly smiled before she too turned and walked away. When she walked past the paintings hung on the walls, they came to life.

The petals, leaves, and stems reached out from the

frames and spread up the walls. Peonies, baby's breath, violet hydrangeas, and red roses blooming followed Gwen. Gwen's heart burned in her chest. She stopped and placed her hand over her heart. When she continued walking, the flowers slowly opened their petals. She could hear her heart beating in her ears. Behind Gwen, roses grew from the floor sprouting and budding as they did. Lush pink petals appeared, shimmered, and turned into butterflies.

When Gwen reached her bedroom door, flowers spread across the wooden door. Gwen pushed it open, and the butterflies fluttered inside ahead of her. Slowly, she closed the door. Through the open balcony doors, the wind from the sea gently brushed the petals of the roses in her room. A finch chirped and flapped its wings as it landed on the balcony rail before a scarlet sun.

Inside her room, Gwen walked around the bed, sat down and looked out at the cerulean sea. From the corner of her eye, she glimpsed something green. Gwen looked over to see a book sitting on her nightstand. The cover seemed to come to life writing G-w-e-n in metallic gold ink.

Gwen picked up the book and laid it on her lap. The cover flipped open, and the pages rustled, turning themselves. The sun was setting over the horizon and the remaining daylight shined on Gwen and the book. As she watched the book her irises turned from jade into luminous pink roses.

Suddenly, the turning pages stopped. A pink butterfly fluttered over to land on the page. Ink appeared bleeding through the pages as Gwen's eyes returned to green. She held the book in both hands as she read a poem called *The Flower*. Alone and in the dark, the flower was saved, revived by a bee. She looked up as her eyes overflowed making small puddles on the page.

When she looked down at the book again a

moment later, the butterfly was gone. A honeybee had taken its place on the page. Its wings vibrated and the bee buzzed away. A teardrop fell blotting out a word of the poem. Soon her tears had washed all the poem away. Gwen sighed heavily, her heart bursting.

The sun set and Gwen was greeted by starlight. She slowly closed the book and walking over to the bookshelf placed the green book on it, her heart all aglow. She opened the balcony doors allowing the bee to disappear into the night. The stars glittered; their reflections painted on the water as Gwen looked out at the sea.

She walked back inside her room, closed the balcony doors and laid down on her bed. Gwen's bedroom door opened. Vines twisted their way inside and spread across Gwen's walls. Peonies, baby's breath, violet hydrangeas, and red roses blossomed all around her room. Gwen sighed heavily and fell into a sound sleep.

The next morning Snow stood beside Gwen purring. She slowly opened her eyes to see the cat kneading the blanket.

"Mmm. Good morning," she muttered.

She reached for the cat and drew him to her. He curled his head into her chest purring and kneading. Gwen kissed his forehead and rubbed her nose on his. She looked up to see the rising sun. The flowers were gone. Through the glass, Gwen saw a robin singing under the aquamarine sky. The bird stood on the balcony rails while big white clouds floated by.

"What time is it?" Gwen gasped and quickly sat up on her bed.

She placed Snow next to her while she changed out of her night gown into her armor. Gwen opened the balcony doors and stepped outside. The robin rose taking flight and soaring across the beach. A clipper ship was waiting just beyond the sand.

"It's time to go," she said.

She turned and looked at Snow sitting on the bed purring.

"Oh Snow, I can't take you with me. I love you. I'll be back before you know it."

Gwen picked the cat up, hugged him and kissed the kitty on his cheek. She placed Snow back on the bed and ran out of the room. Down the hall she ran through a door and followed the staircase going up where she noticed a glass door with steps outside. She opened the door and hurried down a spiraling stone staircase. Gwen ran outside, past the towers, and down another set of stairs. Snow ran down the staircase following her.

The sun was peeking over the castle's wall when she reached the bottom. Gwen ran out into the grass, around the garden, and past the greenhouse. The hin were boarding the ship as it rocked in the water.

"Wait!" she hollered.

She ran up the gangway onto the ship and to the bridge. Harry cranked the planks up when she crossed, and the ship sailed out onto the water.

***

In the main hall, the Prince was looking for Gwen. He roamed the halls stopping to ask each guard if they had seen her. But they all said no. Nicholas found Gwen's door wide open. The morning light shined through the doorway as the Prince approached.

"Gwen?" he called.

Nicholas looked inside the room to see the tangled sheets and the comforter thrown back. Looking up he spotted the clipper ship and ran from the room and down the hallway. The sun was over the horizon. The ship was already moving out to sea.

"Gwen!" he shouted, running from the castle.

At the stables, he untied Sheamus and swung himself onto the horse. The Prince lifted the reins, and they galloped past the castle rushing through the lavender fields to the shore. The waves brushed over the horse's shoes while Nicholas looked out at the ship. It was too far out. He turned the horse around and galloped back to the castle.

***

"Good morning," she said greeting the hin before turning to Phobe. "Phoebe, you came."

The bard looked out over the edge. "I told you I would," she said with a smile.

Gwen walked across the deck and noticed the cat.

"Snow, I told you; you couldn't come," she said.

The cat rubbed himself against her legs waving his fluffy gray tail. Beyond the billowing sails, she saw Fitz standing at the helm.

"Thank you for coming Fitz! Will you be the captain of our ship this morning?" Gwen asked.

"Of course. I hope you don't get seasick! It's going to be a long ride," the halfling said holding the helm with both hands.

He looked over the wheel as the ship glided over the water. The sun glinted off Gwen's armor and warmed the wooden deck as the wind filled the canvas sails.

"Whoo, hot day today!" Haggis shouted from high in the crow's nest.

Sweat glistened and dripped down his face and beard. Harry and Fitz pulled on the rigging adjusting the sails and the ship gathered speed. Gwen looked out across the sea at the castle fading away in the distance.

Fitz stomped over the deck to Gwen. He was carrying a scroll. He unrolled it revealing a map and held it out.

"Looks like we're traveling past the wetlands," he shouted over the wind. The ink appeared to shimmer in silver on the map before it darkened to black.

"How long will we be sailing?" Gwen asked, the wind rushing through her hair.

"It's going to take days, maybe longer. It depends on the weather."

The trees on the map took on a green metallic shimmer.

"Is that where it is?" she asked.

"Yes, it's a long haul past the hills and swamps," the halfling answered.

Gwen, Snow, and the hin floated past the mountains' reflection on the water. The kingdom opened into long wide fields and grassy hills. The ship sailed past a field of grazing sheep. The breeze cooled as the sea opened into a vast blue that reached the horizon.

They sailed *The Fishermen Sea* for days and nights watching peach and lilac sunsets and luminous starlight. One day the wind blew, and raindrops began to fall, but the waters remained calm. Gwen and the hin took shelter in the lower deck. Gwen watched the rain fall through the ship's window, closed her eyes, and drifted away with the sea.

CHAPTER 13
TALE OF THE FISHERMEN SEA

The Prince, handsome in his armor, watched the ocean waves crashing on the shore and foaming against the wizard's feet. Leux stood on the beach holding his staff and watching the water. The Prince walking against a stiff wind approached Leux from behind to stand by his side.

"Why are you standing on the beach?" Nicholas asked.

"Dangers coming," the wizard said, looking at the gray clouds in the dark sky.

"What kind of danger?"

"Sea levels are rising," he said, looking at the Prince.

A sudden gust of wind blew the wizard's hat from his hand.

"I'll go and warn them," the Prince shouted above the sound of the wind.

Nicholas turned, running up the sand onto the grass and into the nearby forest. On the beach, the wizard retrieved his hat as the waves grew and crashed with a roar on the shore. White foam spread over the wizard's feet, beyond the sand and the grass into the lavender fields. He turned around and walked out of the water. Whitecaps rode the turquoise waters that rose as tall as the castle. Through the transparent waters he sighted a creature with greenish gray skin, a colossal head and bluish suckers. Looking up at the creature, Leux tightened his hold on his quarterstaff and slammed it on the sand. A blue topaz light shined brightly atop his staff and a force field appeared out of the ground shielding the shore. The water circled back out to sea.

***

Far out to sea, Gwen and the hin walked the deck under swirling solar flares that reflected bright white light off Gwen's boots. A fish jumped out of the water, its scales glimmering in the sun as seagulls squawked in the distance. A wave rocked the ship. Gwen looked out over the rail at the water, watching the growing waves that lifted the ship.

"Hey! There's something under the ship!" she shouted.

The hin ran over to see a dark shadow below the surface. Harry looked out at the sea. Haggis nearly fell out of the crow's nest with the next wave.

"Kraken!" he shouted the alarm.

The hin scattered over the boat. Some drew their swords while others ran to the lower deck. Fitz ran across the ship to the helm.

"Hold fast the rudder!" he shouted.

Under the deck, the hin opened gunports and pushed cannons into place. They loaded the cannons with shot and powder. Far above, Haggis climbed out of the crow's nest and slid down the rigging onto the deck. As he ran across the deck, he picked up Snow and put the cat inside an empty barrel.

"Sorry kitty," he said, closing the lid.

He dropped the barrel into the water. Fitz was busy putting guns in the hands of the hin. The barrels slipped overboard and rolled off to sea. Long green-gray tentacles reached up the sides of the ship, over the rail and into the gun ports. The hin swarmed over the deck, pushing Gwen into the middle of the ship, taking aim at the climbing tentacles. The kraken's slimy skin glistened in the sun and its suckers popped loudly against the creaking wood.

"Shhh, everyone be still," Harry ordered.

Everyone kept quiet, listening to the creature's suckers pop on and off the wood. Its tentacles reached the top deck.

"Fire!" Fitz shouted.

Cannons and guns blazed. The bullets riddled the kraken's flesh, and the cannon balls burned its tentacles. It drew its arms back into the water. The hin looked over the side at the subsiding waves.

"Hey! I think it's—" Haggis shouted.

The kraken's tentacles shot out of the water first snatching the halfling's stumpy body and then snatching Phoebe lifting them screaming into the sky. More tentacles were climbing high above the ship others reached inside the lower deck. The kraken's tentacles slammed down, breaking the beams and barrels.

"Not the beer!" Harry cried as the monster's tentacles smashed crates open and the gold liquid poured onto the ship's floor.

Harry ran up the wooden steps as the kraken smashed the stairs behind him. Tentacles wrapped around the halfling's ankle and dragged him shouting across the floor. The halfling swept across the broken wood. He reached for a broken beam. His arm slammed against it and Harry screamed in pain. The kraken pulled him through the broken window, cutting his hand and whipping the halfling in the air.

The ship began filling with water. On the top deck, Gwen saw the ship was sinking.

Fitz shouted as he ran across the deck and jumped over the starboard rail into the sea. The kraken's tentacles spread across the deck and snapped the rigging. The ropes dropped down onto the deck. The kraken wrapped a tenacle around a mast.

A fire burned and black smoke spread across the

deck. Gwen, her face covered with soot, drew her sword as the water swept across her boots. The kraken broke through the surface of the sea. Its large, wide charcoal head rose above the ship. Gwen clenched her teeth, held her sword high and charged the kraken with a shout. She jumped up onto the gunwale and off the side of the ship. The creature's eyes were as blue as the sea with wide black pupils. Gwen held her sword in front of her. As the monster lifted its colossal head, water cascaded down its face. The giant octopus rose higher, and Gwen planted her feet on its head. The kraken's head blocked out the sun. The sea monster opened its fang-filled mouth. The kraken loosed a ghastly roar. The hin screamed waving their arms.

The kraken jerked Gwen from its head and lifted Harry higher then sent him plummeting through the air. He glided past Gwen kicking and screaming. She landed back on the kraken's head. Lifting her sword high above her head, she struck the octopus, piercing the kraken's skull. The octopus' screech echoed across the sea. Gwen gripped her sword in both hands and with a grunt twisted it inside the kraken's brain. The creature screamed again. Placing her heel on the hilt, she pushed her sword deeper.

The blade dripped in gray goo when Gwen pulled it out of the kraken's brain. She slid the sword back into the scabbard and jumped off the kraken's head into the sea, swimming against the tide toward the ship. The dead kraken lay in the water, lifeless eyes fixed on the blue sky and its tentacles helplessly floating in the sun before sinking back into the sea.

In the distance, the ship disappeared beneath the waves. Gwen spotted Fitz as the halfling bobbed on the surface. She swam over, wrapped her arm around his waist, and hauled him over to a barrel. Haggis was face down in the water. Gwen reached for another barrel and kicked over to him. She turned the halfling onto his back. His eyes were closed, and he wasn't breathing. Gwen wrapped her arms around the halfling's belly and squeezed. Water spurted from his mouth and Haggis coughed up more. She pulled him onto a floating barrel.

"Gwen!" the bard shouted as she swam up behind Gwen.

"Phoebe! I'm glad you're okay. Help me find the hin."

"Hiya!" Harry said, looking out from inside a nearby barrel.

Gwen looked around and saw the other barrels floating away. There was no land in sight.

"We sunk our ship and now we're lost," Harry said.

The barrels bobbed along carried by the current. Fitz worked his way inside the barrel he was riding.

"Haggis! Haggis, wake up!" Harry shouted at his fellow halfling.

Haggis coughed and opened his eyes "Where are we? What happened?" Haggis asked.

"The kraken sunk our ship. We hoped you knew where we are." Harry said.

"I'm afraid I don't," Haggis replied.

"Lost, we're lost," Harry shouted.

Suddenly, the barrels began to spin and move in a circle.

"Ahhhh! Whirlpool, hold onto your barrels!" Haggis shouted.

Gwen grabbed hold of a barrel and pushed her legs inside. She shot free of the whirlpool. One by one the others followed. Freed of the menacing spinning waters, they spotted land. Harry reached out for a tree branch that floated by. The branch raked along his arm leaving a trail of blood. The blood mixed with the water and a moment later fins broke the surface nearby.

"Sharks!" Phobe shouted, pointing at the fins.

The current slowed but barrels continued moving

toward land aided by the paddling of the riders. Gwen and the hin entered a channel.

"Dry land at last!" Haggis cheered.

"Let's get to shore," Fitz added.

The hin paddled their barrels through the placid stream. Haggis tipped over, the barrel covering the halflings head. He pushed it off and went splashing to shore. Haggis stepped onto the grass. Fitz's barrel rocked up against the dirt and grass. Haggis offered his hand and pulled Fitz out. Harry pushed through the water holding his wounded arm. Haggis took Harry's good hand and pulled him up onto land. Harry grunted with pain, blood seeping through his fingers.

"He's injured," Fitz said.

He was looking at Harry's arm when a barrel passed and brushed up onto the grass. Gwen arrived next and abandoned her barrel for the sun warmed grass.

"Ah," Harry grunted.

"Your arm is broken," Fitz told him.

"I'll be fine," Harry insisted.

"Wha- whoa!" the bard said, teetering on the rim of her barrel.

The bard jumped from the barrel onto the grass where, a few feet away, another barrel lay in the grass. Something inside was scratching at the wood. Haggis walked over to the barrel and heard a meow. He opened the lid and looked inside. Snow was lying inside and meowed again.

"Ah there ya are Snow. You made it," Haggis said.

Gwen walked over to her cat. "Come Snow," she called, reaching inside to pick up the kitty.

"Does anyone know where we are?" Gwen asked.

Fitz reached into his pocket and took out the sopping wet map.

"Oh no, the map is ruined," Gwen said.

"Now how are we going to get back home?" Harry asked.

"We'll have to find another way," Fitz said unrolling the map.

To their surprise, the map dried itself in an instant.

"Hmm," Fitz said, looking down in awe at the dry map. He studied it a moment before walking off through the grass.

"Well, Hmm," Fitz said, clearing his throat.

"It appears we've veered off in the wrong direction. Not to worry. It shouldn't be too hard to find our way," he said.

"Well, where are we?" Harry asked.

"Hmm yes. Well, it appears we need to be on the other side of those hills. I say we head this way," Fitz said, pointing and walking in that direction.

The others fell in behind him and followed him into a forest. They hadn't gone far when the way grew dim.

"Looks like the sun is about to set. Maybe we should take a rest," Fitz said.

"Where will we sleep?" Gwen asked.

"Under any good ole tree will do," Fitz told her.

Phoebe walked over to sit under a prickly pine. "The shade is nice and cool," she declared.

The light shifted into sepia as the sun dropped to the treetops. When the sun was fully set, the hin slept. Haggis spread out in the grass, Harry below a sycamore tree with Fitz on the other side of the trunk. Gwen laid under an ash tree; Snow curled up by her head. The night was still except for the hin snoring.

Gwen didn't sleep. She watched the trees and leaves and thought about Prince Nicholas. She looked up through the leaves at the stars while a gentle breeze blew. Memories played in Gwen's mind. She remembered how the Prince looked at her, how he blushed, smiled, and gazed at her. She remembered Nicholas bringing her coffee and realized she loved him. Her jade eyes filled with tears.

How can this be happening? I told myself I would

never love again. I wasn't looking for Nicholas. I was fine being alone. I never want to go through what I did with Daniel ever again. I never want to experience that kind of pain ever again. The Prince could destroy me, he could break my heart. Nicholas is kind, caring, and considerate. No one has ever been so nice to me. I could be wrong. I could be making a mistake. He has the power to destroy me. But I miss him. I love him. Maybe, just maybe he's the one. But he can only be the one, if he wants to be the one. I've never felt like this before. I love Nicholas with all my heart, she thought.

"I love you Nicholas," Gwen whispered, still looking up at the shimmering stars.

She lay under the ash tree and fell asleep.

CHAPTER 14
BOOK OF SHADOWS

The next morning, Phoebe awoke before the others. The bard sat under the tree as she played her flute soft and quiet. The melody was like a lullaby that soothed the hin while they slept. The music, airy and poetic, carried throughout the woods. Deep in the forest a light fog hung amid the trees. Elk lifted their heads looking up with shining yellow eyes as the music echoed by. The symphony awoke the birds from their nests who began to tweet. Serenity seemed to spread across the land.

Phoebe closed her eyes playing as the birds chirped. The music created a magic sort of sparkling that floated around her. The bard looked up in wonder and smiled, admiring the forest's beauty. Snow awoke from his sleep, lifted his head, and purred while listening to the music. The bard held her flute higher as she played for him.

Gwen slowly opened her eyes. "That sounds so beautiful." she whispered softly.

"Good morning, Gwen. How was your rest?" the bard asked.

"Much needed."

The halflings began awaking and Phoebe put her flute away.

"What's this around my arm?" Harry asked as he sat up in the grass.

His arm was covered with leaves.

"While you were sleeping, I weaved you a sling."

Phoebe said.

"Why did you do that?" the halfling complained.

Fitz and Haggis awoke next.

"Another day, another morning." Fitz said.

Haggis yawned loudly and scratched his beard. Fitz stood up and stretched under the sycamore tree.

"Well, we best get going. We have a long way ahead." Fitz said.

"How 'bout some breakfast?" Harry asked.

"And what do you propose we have?" Fitz asked.

"How about some fish," Harry said.

"I am not going back by the water. Help yourself if you wish," Fitz insisted.

"Perhaps we'll find some food along the way," Haggis assured them.

Gwen, Snow, and the hin started deeper into the forest. By noon, the sky turned crystalline blue.

"I've never been to this part of the woods before," Phoebe said.

"Neither have I," Haggis responded.

They walked past some shrubs and brambles when Fitz called out.

"Hey Harry, there might be some berries to eat over here."

"You think some tiny berries are going to fill us? You've got to be out of your halfling mind," he complained.

"You said you were hungry," Fitz said.

"No berries, they aren't food. Meat is food," Harry argued.

"Take it or leave it." Fitz said.

Harry looked at Fitz and complained under his breath. He searched the bushes pushing aside the leaves and discovered plump round gooseberries. He plucked them from their stems and started eating them.

"Hey! These berries are good and sweet. Come have some. There's plenty to go around." Harry said excitedly.

He ate the berries letting the juices drip down his chin. The hin accepted Harry's offer and gathered around the bush picking berries. Suddenly, they heard something stomp the ground.

"What was that?" Haggis asked.

"Many creatures live in this forest. Don't worry." Fitz assured them.

They continued eating when Gwen noticed strange markings on the bark of a tree. "Hey, what are these markings?" she asked.

Haggis walked up next to Gwen taking a look. "Oh no! Stop eating the berries! We must leave!" He exclaimed.

"What is it, Haggis?" Fitz asked.

"These are the markings of an owl bear," he warned.

"We'd best be going. Hurry!" Fitz shouted.

He dropped the berries on the ground and ran. Harry shoved more berries into his mouth filling his plump cheeks and followed. They all ran through the forest until they saw a tiny creature sitting in the grass. Fitz stuck out his arm, signaling for everyone to stop. Gwen came to a halt just behind Fitz's elbow. She saw what appeared to be a bear cub with the face of an owl. The animal looked up at the group with its big yellow eyes and blinked. It tilted its head and opened its tiny beak in a yawn.

"That's what you're worried about?" Gwen asked.

"Shhh, be very quiet. Don't be fooled." Fitz whispered.

The rest of the hin stood still watching the creature. It had both fur and feathers in yellow and brown. It had bear paws and its belly was ivory with small brown feathers. The animal's pointed ears flared out above its head.

The baby turned its neck, looking nearly backward and hooted. When it did, something big and brown crawled from the bushes. It walked on all fours, its large paws sinking into the soil. The baby's mother rose up onto its back legs. It was as large and tall as a bear, but its face was that of an owl. The carnivorous owl bear opened its beak in a screeching roar. The group ran, the mother chased after them on all fours.

The owl bear pounced landing between the hin and the baby. The owl bear growled and swiped its claws at the hin. The group stopped and slowly backed away. The mother snapped its ivory beak and released a stunning screech. The hin quickly covered their ears in pain. Blood streamed from their ears and down the sides of their heads.

The owl bear charged the hin galloping across the grass. Gwen ran up a tree and knelt down on a branch. As the owl bear ran by, she dropped onto its back, grabbing hold of its feathers. The creature arched its back and kicked its back legs. Gwen held on as it rushed past the trees, She was quickly approaching a long branch. She ducked down as it flew past her head. The hin scattered in all directions.

Haggis looked back over his shoulder. The owl bear was going after Harry. The halfling screamed as he ran around a tree. The bear's feet dug up the dirt as it swung around, Gwen still holding on and tugging on its feathers. The owl bear turned its head all the way around. Its large yellow eyes stared at Gwen. Its face was angry. It stood and started clawing at its back. Gwen reached up, grabbing hold of a branch. It clawed Gwen legs as she lifted herself into the tree and began climbing higher.

The owl bear jumped for her, missed and dropped back to the ground. It then began shaking the tree. Gwen leaped across onto another tree. The owl bear growled and turned feasting its eyes on Fitz. The halfling stood in the center of a path.

"If you don't kill her, she'll have us all for lunch," the halfling cried.

Gwen looked out at the baby. She watched the cub roll onto its belly and walk on all fours.

"No, climb a tree!" Gwen shouted.

"Are you out of your mind?" Fitz yelled.

"Everyone, climb a tree!" Gwen shouted across the forest.

Fitz looked up at the owl bear. Its eyes were fixed on the halfling. Fitz turned and ran. He wrapped his arms around a tree, quickly pulling himself up. Phoebe's eyes searched the forest in a panic. She spotted a tree with a low branch. She grabbed onto it, lifted her short legs, and walked up the side of the trunk. The other halflings also climbed trees. The owl bear roared again. When the owl bear stopped screaming, it looked down at its offspring. It turned, got back down on all fours, and walked back into the forest with its baby following behind.

Gwen breathed heavily as she looked down and watched the animals leave. When they were gone, she dropped from the tree. Fitz, Harry, and Haggis climbed down. Phoebe saw Snow above her on another branch. She climbed up to cradle the cat under her arm. Gwen walked over to wait at the bottom of the tree. Phoebe lowered the cat to Gwen.

"It's okay Snow. You're safe now," she said as she held him close.

"What did you let it go for?" Haggis demanded.

"It's a mother. I couldn't leave a baby without its mother," Gwen said.

"Are you out of your bloody mind?" Harry berated.

"No, I'm not. We're all safe now," Gwen said with a smile.

"No thanks to you," Harry rebuked.

"Shall we continue?" Fitz said as he wiped the dirt and dust from his clothes.

"What choice do we have?! I'm not staying here to be that owl bear's dinner," Harry's replied.

"Very well then. Let's get a move on." Fitz told

them.

They continued down the path. The sea was now far behind them. As they looked out on the hills far in the distance, it started to rain.

"Oh great. Just what we need. Rain," Harry complained.

"You're welcome to find yourself shelter Harry." Fitz grinned at the halfling's grumbling.

"Not a very happy hin today are we," Phoebe commented.

"No, and who would be? I want to go home to my brewery!" Harry whined.

"Oh Harry. How will you ever survive?" Phoebe said and chuckled.

Fitz took out his map, unrolled it and held it up to read the shimmering silver ink that reappeared. The parchment drew an image of a weeping willow, and the ink shined green. A wide grin spread across Fitz's face.

"What? What are you smiling about?" Harry demanded.

Fitz nodded his head and pointed his finger. "There, up ahead. That's the tree," he said.

"Ah finally. Now we can go home," Harry said.

"Not quite." Fitz winked at the halfling as he rolled the scroll and put it back into his pocket.

As the quiet rain fell from the gray sky, Gwen and the hin walked towards the tree. Soon they were gathered beneath the weeping willow.

"Where's the book?" Haggis asked.

"Oh now, you didn't think it would be that easy, did you?" Fitz asked.

"Of course not," Gwen said looking up at the tree and touching the bark. "Why would the book just be laying under the tree. Then anyone could come and take it. We have to dig for it." Gwen said.

"Dig? But we don't have shovels," Harry groused.

"Well then I guess we'll just have to use our hands," Fitz said.

Gwen placed Snow on the ground. They all got down on their hands and knees and dug through the mud in the rain as lightning flashed. They dug and dug until their arms and hands were covered in the sludge. Gwen wiped the rain from her face with her shoulder. Then, she felt something hard under the mud. The rain washed the surface revealing something black beneath. She placed it in the wet grass and rubbed her bare hands over it. S-h-a appeared in gold letters. She wiped away more of the mud. It was a thick black book. At the top of the book was a gold pentacle. In a golden frame were the words *Book of Shadows*.

Gwen looked at the book in amazement. "Guys! I got it! I found the book!"

Suddenly all was quiet.

"Guys?" She said, looking up.

Snow and the hin were frozen in place. Phoebe sat on her knees. Fitz was on his knees reaching out to Haggis who sat in front of him. Harry stood angrily with his arms crossed. The rain falling from the sky was also suspended, the droplets shining like crystals. She touched a droplet in front of her and it turned to water.

Gwen looked down at the book, opened the cover, and turned the pages. The ground around her shook as the roots of the tree broke through the ground. The slender branches rose, their leaves spreading out over Gwen's head. Forming themselves into the walls of the crone's cottage. Suddenly, Gwen found herself in the crone's kitchen holding the book as the cottage rose into the air.

"Hey! Where'd she go?" Harry asked.

"Where's the tree?" Haggis shouted.

In the cottage kitchen, Gwen gasped. She was all alone– just her and the book.

CHAPTER 15
CURSE OF THE SWAMP HAG

G wen looked out the kitchen window. The rain stopped. The cottage floated high in the forest. She could see the hin standing around in a state of confusion. Without warning the shutters slammed shut blocking out the light from outside. The interior of the cottage was dimly lit as the sigils and words on the book's pages glowed bright purple. The light shined on Gwen's face as she flipped through the pages searching for the spell.

She read the titles: Mind On Fire, Witches Storm, and Veil of Death. Gwen flipped more pages, and she found it. Souls Resurrection, the words shimmered at the top of the page. She knew nothing about magic, especially black magic.

"If this is the spell the crone cast to reincarnate herself, then what spell will break it?" she asked herself.

She read the list of tools and ingredients: apple, juice from a lemon, a pinch of salt, dash of black pepper, dash of Cayenne pepper, three drops of witch hazel, a single drop of blood. One red candle, one purple candle, one black candle, one green candle, one white candle. Gwen searched the kitchen for what she needed. She found salt, black pepper, and cayenne in the cabinets. She placed the book down, grabbed the spices, and placed them on the counter. She walked across the kitchen into the pantry. There she found a basket of red apples and a bowl full of lemons. She carried the fruit as she searched for the witch hazel.

"Witch hazel," she whispered.

She searched the pantries shelves but there were no oils or potions. Walking out of the pantry, she noticed shelves on the wall next to the cauldron. She walked over and read the labels.

"Ugh, it's not here either."

She walked to another set of shelves across the room. Lavender, juniper berries, rose buds, and finally witch hazel. She grabbed the small bottle as she walked back to the counter. She opened a cabinet and took out a mortar and pestle.

She placed the apple whole inside of the bowl. Then she sprinkled salt, pepper, and cayenne.

"Knife. I need a knife," she said to herself.

She looked around and finally found the drawer with the knives.

"Okay. Just a single drop," she whispered.

She pointed the knife at her fingertip and lightly poked it. She rushed over to the mortar and squeezed her finger. A single drop fell on the apple. She sliced the lemon down the middle and squeezed half of the lemon into the bowl. After three drops of witch hazel, she walked back inside the pantry and grabbed a pillar candle of each color.

Gwen placed the mortar in the center of the table. She arranged the candles in the shape of a star around the bowl in the order the book listed them.

"How will I light them?"

She walked to the counter and got the book and laid it before the makeshift altar. The candles suddenly ignited by themselves.

"That works." She nervously sighed. "Come on Gwen think. What should I chant?" she asked.

That was when Gwen remembered Sinnafain and how when she bestowed Gwen's armor her eyes changed from green to gold.

"She filled me with magic," Gwen muttered.

She looked down at the glowing book and the words floated off the paper. Gwen's eyes turned into bright green lights. Gwen rose to hover a foot above the wooden floor as knowledge filled her. Gwen's eyes glowed as she spoke.

From dusk to dawn
This creature's soul
Dares evil spawn
From down below.

Witches rebirth,
The wretched crone
From powered Earth
And aching bones.

Her voice deepened as she recited the incantation, and the table began to shake. Gwen's hair floated away from her head and the mortar vibrated on the wooden table. Gwen's belly grew, protruding as if she was pregnant. Her armor expanded with her. The crone's face formed pushing against the metal. She was trapped inside Gwen. The witch screamed and wailed. Spiders emerged from the ceiling and scattered across the walls.

The crone continued to push her face against Gwen's abdomen. Gwen's body gave off a violet aura. She looked back at the book and began the chant again.

From dusk to dawn
This creature's soul
Dares evil spawn.
From down below

Witches rebirth,
The wretched crone
From powered Earth

And aching bones.

Evil now dies,
Permanent sleep.
Bellows she cries
Tortured and weak.

Magic destroyed,
Her spell I break.
Into the void
Never to wake.

Spirits arise,
Death set us free.
All seeing eye,
So mote it be.

The candles' flames fluttered with the words. The table stopped shaking and the altar steadied. Gwen's stomach deflated and the crone's wailing stopped. The violet aura that surrounded Gwen faded. Inside the mortar, the apple changed from red into a deep dark purple. All of a sudden, the crone's ghost emerged from the floor. Gwen's eyes widened as she looked at the wispy apparition. The crone rose towards the ceiling, looking down at Gwen with her black empty eye sockets. The ghost cried as black tears streamed and dripped down her face. When the scream died away, she knelt down and picked the book up.

The crone flew toward Gwen who ducked letting the spirit pass over her head. The crone disappeared into the wall. Gwen turned back towards the altar and saw a black hooded reaper standing on the other side of the table. Gwen looked at death as death looked at her. It lifted its arm and pointed its bony finger at the wall. She turned to look, and the cottage filled with light. Gwen looked back and the reaper was gone.

The book in her arms was closed and no longer

glowing. Gwen could hear the birds chirping outside. She walked around the table, and the cottage started shaking. The floor broke into roots. The walls turned back into willow branches that waved as they spread apart. The ceiling shook sending debris crashing down. Gwen ran to the door, opened it and found herself standing high in the forest among all the other trees. The floor continued breaking apart. Gwen placed her hand on the door frame while watching behind her.

She held the book close to her chest and stepped over the edge. She closed her eyes, blinked, and reappeared on the ground.

"Gwen! Where did you go?" Haggis asked.

"She did it. She broke the spell." Fitz said.

She looked and the tree was gone. "Where's the weeping willow?" she asked.

"The spell is broken. You destroyed the crone and her magic. The cottage is gone." Fitz said.

"It's finally over." Gwen smiled in relief.

"Let's go home." Fitz said pursing his mouth.

Gwen, Snow, and the hin continued their journey. Gwen carried the book as they walked.

"It's strange you know," Gwen remarked.

"What is?" Haggis asked.

"Well the last time I met the crone, the cottage was in the swamp."

"The cottage hasn't moved dear. It's always been outside of the swamp." Fitz said.

"You know...now that I think of it, you're right. It must have been because I walked through the swamp at night. The cottage was hidden behind some bushes." Gwen recalled.

"And it is the swamp we have to walk in order to return home," Fitz announced.

"Do we have to walk through the dirty old swamp? Isn't there another way?" Harry asked.

"No Harry, it's the only way. Unless you want to

swim across the sea," Fitz answered the halfling's grumbling.

After a time, they came to a lake with a thin mist that rode on the water. The crystal waters reflected the trees in a mirror image.

"Ah come on! There has to be a way around!" Harry complained.

"There is. We don't have to walk through the water. Follow me." Fitz said.

They made their way past the sedges and immense bulrushes. The wetlands darkened as they walked under the shaded trees and entered the swamp.

"It's much bigger than I remember," Gwen said.

"The swamp is huge," Fitz told her walking past a puddle of oozing mud. "Watch your step."

The group continued past a channel surrounded by twisting branches, draped in Spanish moss that arched above the water. The long channel spread far out into an opening. Dead stumps coated in moss and algae were scattered across the bogs. Deeper into the swamp there were slow flowing streams, and larger trees.

"Help!" a voice called.

Phoebe gasped. "What was that?"

"Help!" the sweet voice of a female called again.

"Do you guys hear that?" Phobe asked.

"Help!"

"Someone's in danger!" Haggis exclaimed.

"That voice, I know that voice," Gwen uttered. "Madeleine? No, it can't possibly..." Gwen shook her head in confusion.

"That is Madeleine," Haggis agreed.

"It can't be, Madeleine's dead," Harry said.

"Or is she..." Fitz remarked.

"What do you mean or is she? We should know. We made her memorial," Harry argued.

"Perhaps. But the hobs only found a skeleton in the woods. Who's to say it was Madeleine? It could have been anyone," Fitz said.

"Why would the hobs bring someone else's skeleton into the castle?" Harry asked.

"Well, they are goblins. Look, all I'm saying is that no one actually saw Madeleine. There's a chance it could have been someone else," Fitz explained as the woman screamed again.

"No, I won't listen to this. Madeleine is gone. She wouldn't just disappear," Harry assured them.

"Maybe she didn't. Maybe she got lost or maybe someone kidnapped her," Phoebe suggested.

"Oh, bloody hell!" Harry fumed.

The group proceeded with caution further into the swamp. They looked around but didn't see anyone.

"Well it's gone now," Harry said.

"I know what I heard. Phoebe, do you know what you heard?" Fitz asked.

"I do. I heard Madeleine. I say we don't give up until we find her. For all we know she may still be alive," Phoebe replied.

The group grew quiet when they heard footsteps sloshing through the swamp. The group went silent. A few feet away, a green creature walked out from behind the trees. It paid no mind to Gwen or the hin. It was dragging Madeleine by her hair across the dirt and mud.

"Let me go! Let me go!" she cried.

The naked creature had green clammy skin and sagging tubular breasts. Its raven black hair was long and thin reaching all the way down the creature's back. Spanish moss dangled down its arms.

"Ahhhhh!" the gardener screamed.

"Hey! Let her go!" Gwen shouted, giving Fitz the book and going after Madeleine.

The creature ignored her, continuing to drag Madeleine. The hin and Phoebe carrying Snow ran after Gwen. As Gwen got closer, the gardener reached out her hand for help.

"Help me! Please!" she cried.

Gwen still couldn't see her face. Madeleine's hair dangled in front of her.

"Let her go," Gwen demanded.

The creature stopped and Madeleine stopped kicking. The creature slowly turned to look at Gwen with its pale-yellow eyes.

"What the—" Gwen muttered.

Madeleine disappeared. The hin suddenly found their feet glued in the mud.

"Gwen!" Phoebe cried.

Gwen looked back. They were unable to move.

"Where'd she go? Where's Madeleine?" Gwen demanded.

The dewy creature opened its mouth revealing her long sharp teeth. Her face was wrinkled with a wart on the side of her chin, her nose long and pointed.

"What did you do with Madeleine?" Gwen insisted.

The hag hissed and she grabbed Gwen by her neck. Her long fingers and twisted claws wrapped around Gwen's throat. She lifted Gwen off the ground. Gwen reached for her sword, gasping for air as the hag choked her. Gwen found her sword and drew it. When she did, the creature disappeared, dumping Gwen to the ground. The hin still couldn't move. They grunted with effort trying to lift their legs. Gwen put her sword away and walked back to them.

"Take my hand!" Gwen offered.

As she reached for Phobe, the hag reappeared in front of her. Gwen gasped, falling back and watching from the ground in horror as the hag slowly approached. The hag hissed and snatched the air. Gwen scrabbled up, her armor spreading over her hands. Phoebe started rapidly whispering. She spoke too fast for Gwen to understand, but the hag covered her ears, screaming in pain.

Gwen lifted her arms, her palms out and lightning cracked striking the hag. Her body jolted, shook and disappeared. Gwen lowered her hands and the hag suddenly reappeared grabbing Gwen by the wrist. Gwen tried pulling away, but the hold was too strong. The hag fixed her eyes on Gwen's draining her energy. Gwen weakened and slowly fell to her knees. Tree branches reached up from the shaking ground encircling the hin.

Fitz, Haggis, Harry, and Phoebe watched wide eyed.

"Gwen!" Haggis called.

Gwen looked up, eye lids slowly opening and closing. She placed her hand on her knee and stood up breaking free. The hag's long sharp claw sliced Gwen's cheek. She grabbed the hag's hand pulling it and the hag bit her.

"You wicked wench," Gwen growled infuriated.

The hag smiled. Gwen's head leaned back, and her body rocked. Tentacles emerged from Gwen's mouth, waving in the air above her face. Gwen grabbed onto the tentacles pulling on them. Gwen's pupils became rectangular like the kraken's. She stood looking at the hag as the tentacles waved and twisted before going back inside Gwen's mouth. She closed her lips and her eyes shone neon green.

"You're my slave now." A deep womanly voice spoke from Gwen.

Gwen charged at the hag. The creature only stood there smiling as Madeleine reappeared on the ground at her feet.

"Help me, Gwen. Help me," Madeleine whimpered.

Gwen looked down at the gardener and placed her hand on Madeleine's shoulder. The gardener's face drifted away as smoke, breaking the illusion. Gwen caught the hag by her neck strangling her. The hag started to gag, and Gwen stomped her foot on the ground. Tremors vigorously shook the entire swamp. The waters rippled as a tree broke through the earth's crust. Branches elongated twisting around the hag's slender arms. Her amphibian-like legs changed into bark. The change continued on past her hips. Her hair became branches bearing leaves. Gwen released her grip and stepped back. The hag looked down watching her body and screamed until bark covered her mouth and face. The hag was gone, an elm tree now stood in her place.

Gwen sighed, her eyes returning to jade. She walked to rejoin the group. The cat looked at Gwen and meowed.

"What happened?" the bard asked.

"She's gone," Gwen said.

"What do you mean she's gone? Did you kill her?!" Haggis asked.

"No, I didn't kill her. She's right there," Gwen said looking back over her shoulder.

"Where?" Harry asked, eyes searching.

"Right there. That tree," Gwen answered.

The hin looked at each other in a state of complete and utter confusion.

"I'm just glad she's gone," Phoebe said relieved.

"Show me the way home," Gwen said to Fitz.

"Yes right, can't wait to get there myself," the halfling replied, walking past the hag as they exited the swamp.

"Oh, may I please have the book back?" Gwen asked.

"Yes, of course. I sure don't want it," Fitz said handing it over.

Gwen grinned. "This book needs to be put away somewhere never to be seen ever again."

"Ain't that the truth," Harry agreed.

Gwen looked back at the swamp fading in the distance. They made their way past the marshes when they saw a pond behind the tall grass. A lush green willow grew on the bank and lily pads delicately floated on the water.

"The breeze is quite nice," Fitz said. "Hopefully

there won't be any more monsters."

"I have to say, from what I've learned here nothing surprises me anymore," added Phobe.

"What else could there possibly be?" Gwen asked.

"Oh, you'd be surprised." Fitz replied as Haggis and Harry chuckled.

"What? Did I say something funny?" Gwen asked.

"It's just that when you think you've seen it all, things can still surprise you." Haggis answered.

"I suppose you're right," Gwen said.

"It's a big world out there," Harry added.

The woods opened up and they found themselves standing surrounded by lupines. In the distance they saw the mountains.

"Where are we?" Phoebe asked. "How much further until we reach the castle?"

Fitz reached into both pockets and waddled around in a circle.

"What is it?" Gwen asked.

He looked at the ground. "Well, it...uh." Fitz coughed clearing his throat. "It seems I have...um...lost the map."

"You lost the map?" Harry shouted.

"It was here in my pocket. And well now, it's not."

"Where did you lose it?" Haggis asked.

"If I knew that, we wouldn't have this problem right now," Fitz replied. "I don't know where it went."

"So, we're lost?" Phoebe asked with wide eyes.

"No." Fitz cleared his throat again. "No, we are not lost."

"Then how are we going to find our way back?" Haggis asked.

"Well. if we continue that way then—"

"Then what?" Harry cut him off. "We're lost and have no map.

"I think we'll be fine. All we have to do is continue past the hills and go back through the forest. We'll figure it out from there," Fitz explained.

"You better be right." Harry snapped.

"If I'm not then I'm not," Fitz told him.

Harry looked annoyed. Fitz only smiled. He took his hands out of his pockets, and they continued walking. Trees soon gathered around. They had found their way back into the forest but were growing tired. Haggis stopped and stood with his hands on his knees breathing heavily.

"I think we might need to take another rest. I don't know how much longer I can go on," he said exhausted.

"It doesn't help not having a map," Harry remarked as he started scratching his hands.

Gwen scratched her face. Then, Phoebe started scratching her arms. Snow used his back paws to scratch his head.

"Why are we all scratching?" Gwen asked.

The hin were covered with red patches.

"I think we might have accidentally gotten into something," Gwen said.

"What do you mean?" Phoebe asked, continuing to scratch herself.

"Phoebe, your arms are all red. How's my face?" Gwen asked.

"Oh no, Gwen! Your face is red," she answered.

"Looks like we might have touched some poison oak," Fitz explained as he scratched harder.

Gwen noticed a moss-covered log and went to sit down. Snow jumped up beside her and all the hin took a seat.

"I don't think scratching does much good." Gwen commented.

"I don't care. It itches too much," Harry complained, scratching the back of his head.

All of a sudden, the log shook.

"What is that?" Phoebe said.

Phoebe, Snow, and the hin quickly jumped off the log. Gwen continued to scratch her face when the log lifted off the ground.

"Hey! What's going on!" Gwen shouted.

She placed her hands on the log as she rose higher.

The hin screamed and scrambled away. Gwen looked up and saw the face of a giant green man. He stood as tall as the trees. His body was made of bark and leaves with a broad chest and muscular arms. Moss, vines, and foliage covered him. He had long hair made of leaves and a long matching beard. Smaller trees grew from his curved horns and from his shoulders.

"Are you the green man?" Gwen asked.

"Some call me that. Others call me Terran. I'm the keeper of the forests and the woods," he explained.

The creature lifted his arm so Gwen could look into his big golden eyes.

"I'm sorry, I didn't mean to sit on you," she said.

"That's quite alright. You must be far from home," he replied.

"What makes you say that?" she asked.

"Not many wander out this far. It's not every day I see a human."

"And it's not every day I meet a talking tree," she said.

The giant chuckled. "We're not all that different you know."

"How are we not different? You're made of bark and leaves. You're as tall as the forest," she said.

"Because we all come from nature."

"Good point," Gwen replied.

"What's your name?"

"Gwen. I take it you're not going to eat me or you would have done it by now."

"Eat you? Why would I eat you?" he asked. "Do you think just because I'm large and tall I would eat you?"

"You're right. I've seen a lot of scary things in these woods. Please forgive me," Gwen said.

"Here, sit in my hand," he said, opening his fingers.

Gwen ran down the giant's forearm and stood in the center of his wooden palm.

"You look hurt. What happened to you?" he asked.

"My friends and I got into some poison oak."

Terran lowered his head and took a closer look at Gwen. He noticed the rash on her face and the cut on her cheek. Gwen looked up at the giant as his other hand came down, closing over his palm. Gwen stood inside a sphere. Rays of light shined through the giant's fingers. The giant's hands sprouted green grass. Through the grass came crocuses, snowdrops, and sweet peas. The sphere began spinning and Gwen fell onto a bed of wildflowers. She smiled laughing as the world spun around. The green man lifted his top hand and Gwen looked up at the blue sky. She touched her face with her hand.

"Thank you," she said.

The cut, redness, and the itching were all gone.

"Would you help my friends too?" she asked.

"They all ran off."

"You'll have to forgive them. They're tired and we've been walking for a long time," Gwen said.

"Where are you going?" Terran asked.

"Home. Well, home for them anyways. To the castle," she said.

"You really are far from home. You must be lost."

"Well, we lost our map."

"Not to worry. I can help you get back to the castle," he promised.

"You can! That would be wonderful. I wouldn't be able to thank you enough."

"Of course, it's no problem. May Beltane bless you in many ways Gwen," the green man said as he smiled looking down with his bright golden eyes.

"What do you mean? You're not just a giant are you?" Gwen asked.

Terran looked out into the forest. "I think I see your friends."

He slowly lowered his hand as he carefully placed it on the forest floor. Gwen remained standing in the middle of the green man's palm.

"Guys, it's okay! He won't hurt us!" Gwen shouted. "Come out!"

The hin stepped out from behind the trees.

"Are you sure?" Haggis asked.

"Yes, I'm sure. Everyone, this is Terran. He's going to help us get back home." Gwen smiled.

All of the hin stepped forward approaching the giant's hand. Phoebe carried Snow as they stepped up joining Gwen. The hand lifted them up and the hin looked down at the forest.

"I heard you lost your map. Gwen tells me you halflings need help getting home," Terran said.

"Uh...um yes...if you would be so kind." Fitz stuttered.

The giant's irises and pupils vanished. The wind picked up as the sky turned from blue to gray. The hin struggled to stand against the force of the wind. Terran's hair waved and blew as he looked out across the kingdom. He cupped his hands back together. He covered Snow, Gwen, and all the hin with his hand. This time it was dark in his hands.

"What's going on? What's happening?!" Fitz asked.

"He's going to crush us," Phoebe exclaimed.

Outside the dome, the lightning crackled, and thunder rumbled. Snow leaped out from Phoebe's arms onto the bark of the giant's palm. He ran across the giant's hand disappearing in the darkness.

"Snow!" Gwen cried, running after him.

When the light returned, the hin, Gwen, and Snow all stood looking at each other.

"Your poison oak is gone!" Fitz exclaimed looking at Haggis.

"Yours too. And you too Harry," Haggis said.

"What about me? Is mine gone?" Phoebe asked.

"It is!" Gwen smiled, nodding her head.

The giant was gone, and they were standing in a new part of the forest.

"Where are we?" Haggis asked.

Gwen turned and walked to sit beneath a cherry tree. Snow ran to her and stood at her side. The hin followed the cat to where Gwen sat. They all looked out at a pond with two swans. In the distance, they saw the castle.

"Home." Haggis smiled, stretching his mustache as his face lit up.

CHAPTER 16
THE KEY OF DESTINY

As they made their way past a cedar tree, Gwen placed her hand on the bark and smiled. They were out of the forest at last. The open drawbridge, a welcome sight, was visible though the castle was shrouded in fog. As Snow, Gwen, and the hin crossed it, the guards opened the castle doors. They stood in the entry way for a moment, taking it all in when the Queen approached.

"Ah, you made it. Welcome home." Helena greeted them with a smile. "I didn't think you would make it. Safe travels I hope?"

"Well, not exactly." Fitz said.

"But the good news is that you all made it back in one piece," she said.

"That we did Your Majesty." Haggis took a bow.

"Come, you must be hungry. The hobs will arrange a warm meal for you," she insisted.

"Gwen, your book," Fitz said, lifting the spell book.

"Thank you, thank you all for going with me," she said, taking the book in her arms.

"We couldn't let you go alone. It was too dangerous. We were happy to accompany you," Haggis said.

"I'm just glad we made it home and we didn't lose anyone along the way." Gwen smiled.

"Here, here. Let's eat, I'm starving," Harry said.

"I'll see you all later," Gwen said with a grin. "I'm going to get resettled in my room."

"I'm ravenous. We'll see you later Gwen. You know where to find us." Fitz smiled.

The hin continued down the hall as Gwen walked up the palace steps with Snow right behind her.

"We're home," she said looking down at Snow and smiling.

She turned the knob and walked inside. Gwen saw the cat tree had grown larger. It sprouted roots that lay exposed atop the wooden floor. The top of the tree reached new heights.

"The tree has taken over the whole room. How am I going to get this out of here?" she said.

Snow leaped over Gwen's boots as he sprinted over the roots. He latched his claws into the tree and climbed up.

"Fine, if it makes you happy, we'll keep it." Gwen said with a sigh as Snow smiled with his eyes and started to purr.

She walked across the room and placed the book on the bed before going to the dresser and opening the drawer. She took out the pink box and lifted the lid. She looked at the mirror as it laid face down, grabbed it by the handle, and took it out. She placed the box on top of the dresser, admiring the golden leaves and roses on the back of the mirror. She traced her fingers along the petals and smiled.

Through the balcony doors, she looked out at the sea watching the gentle waves foam and brush over the sand. She could hear the seagulls squawking in the distance. Gwen took a deep breath and released a heavy sigh. She turned the mirror around, holding it up to her face. The glass rippled like raindrops on a pond. Her reflection smiled back at her. But Gwen was not smiling. The key reappeared, shining a bright gold around its tiny diamonds and pink topaz gemstones.

The key suddenly shrunk and appeared as a necklace on Gwen's reflection. Her hand went to her neck, and she felt something there. She placed the mirror face down on the dresser. She looked down at the key she held in her hand. She lifted the golden chain over her head. She held the amulet in her hand rubbing her fingers over it. It was much smaller than when it first appeared. She placed the mirror back in the box, closed the lid, and put it back inside the drawer.

Holding the necklace in her hand, she turned and walked back to the bed. She picked up the spell book, looked for a place to put it. On the shelves, she noticed the green book. She took it out and put the spell book in its place. Her name, written in gold, appeared on the plain green cover.

"You're a tricky little book, aren't you?" she whispered.

A dark keyhole appeared in the middle of the cover. Gwen opened her hand and looked at the key in her palm. Holding it by the crown, inserted the key into the hole. She turned it and the book opened itself. The cover flipped open, and the pages turned. When the pages stopped turning, the words began to form on the empty pages. As they did, Gwen read aloud.

Withered roses, hearts of stone
Wander around lost and alone
Delicate petals, fragile snow
Blush in enchanted afterglow...
... a mate to a soul

The words slowly seeped back into the page. The pages flipped again, and the book closed. Gwen placed it on top of the dresser. She put the key back over her head.

She reflected on the poem. The words touched her. She took a deep breath and when she looked up, the book started changing. A gold frame appeared on the cover. Intricate golden vines weaved themselves together in a whimsical pattern. Flowers bloomed on all four corners. The image of the key emerged under Gwen's name. Mesmerized in wonderment, she watched pink and ivory butterflies appear. They fluttered behind the flowers and became still.

"Sinnafain," Gwen whispered under her breath.

Her eyes widened. She turned and ran out of the room and down the palace steps. Sunlight hit the key, and it shined ever so brightly. When she reached the bottom of the steps, she ran into the Prince.

"Gwen! You made it back. How was your trip?" he asked.

"It was fine. I'm sorry, I have to go!" she exclaimed, rushing past him and out of the castle door.

The Prince shook his head, turned, and walked away.

Gwen ran back down the drawbridge and darted into the forest. She ran past the wisteria tree, and the pond, stopping when reached the waterfall. Bright blue lights appeared sparkling in the air. As Gwen watched the fairies appeared.

"Hello Gwen," Shadow greeted vibrating her wings.

Quildorra appeared next followed by all the other fairies.

"Where's Sinnafain?" Gwen asked.

"I'm right here," the maiden's voice called from a white light. "I've been expecting you."

She gracefully stepped forward as the fairies fluttered around her. "How was your journey?"

"Difficult," Gwen said.

Sinnafain noticed Gwen's necklace. "I see you found the key. Congratulations."

"That's why I came. I was wondering if there's anything you can tell me about it," Gwen said.

The maiden grinned looking up at Gwen. "I've been waiting for you to find it."

"What do you mean?" Gwen asked.

"You may have saved the Prince, but he also saved you," Sinnafain said.

"I don't understand. How did he save me? I didn't need saving." Gwen said.

"Oh, but you did. You broke his curse, and he opened your heart to love again. Finding the key means you have now stepped into your power. It is the key of destiny," the maiden explained.

"The poem..." Gwen whispered as her eyes searched the ground.

"That's right. The key manifested because you have stepped into your destiny. I told you great things awaited you. And this is only the beginning."

Gwen was speechless. She held the key by the chain and looked at it.

"The key is yours to keep. You'll never know when you'll need it," the maiden told her.

"You said this is only the beginning. What do you mean by that?" Gwen asked, releasing the amulet.

"You did well but more awaits you. You still have much to learn. You'll see." Sinnafain smiled. "My dear, you are already blessed. Let go of fear and go where you are guided."

"So that's it? There's nothing else you can teach me?" Gwen asked.

"You already have everything you need. All you have to do is look inside of yourself. If you want to learn, study. If you want to be proficient, practice. My magic is with you," the maiden said, searching Gwen's eyes.

The fairies flew past Gwen and soared over the pond. Gwen watched them disappear behind the waterfall. When she turned back, the maiden was gone. She was alone in the forest.

"She's right. Maybe I just need to believe and trust in myself." Gwen said.

She touched the key on her neck and headed back toward the castle. She closed her eyes going within herself like the maiden told her. She sighed and opened her eyes.

"Whoa!" She exclaimed, looking down. She was standing five feet above the ground. "Okay, her magic *is* always with me. I just need to harness it."

As she continued walking, her footprints shimmered with an iridescent glow. She walked out of the forest and back down to the ground. Returning to the castle, she saw the Queen.

"Your majesty." Gwen bowed her head. "I have a question. It's about the mirror."

"Yes of course. What is it?" the Queen asked.

"I just don't understand," Gwen said shaking her head. "Why didn't the mirror show me what was going to happen to Madeleine? Gwen furrowed her brows in frustration.

"Oh Gwen, my dear..." The Queen paused. "The mirror only shows us what we want to see."

"But it showed me things that hadn't happened yet." Gwen said.

"Yes, it's an oracle like I told you. But the mirror only shows us the good and our hearts desire." The Queen explained.

"I see. I just wish I would have known."

"It's okay. Sometimes we're not meant to know everything," the Queen said.

"I guess you're right."

"Why don't you go rest. I'll have Gerald bring some food up to your room."

"Thank you, Your Majesty." Gwen bowed.

Gwen walked up the palace stairs to her room. After eating, Gwen stood on the balcony and looked out at the sea. The wind brushed her face and tousled through her hair. After a while, she walked back inside and went to bed.

The next day, the sun shined through the windows waking Gwen. She squinted and rolled. Knocking at her door chased sleep far away. She sat up and looked toward the balcony. The sun blinded her, so she got up and walked to the door with her eyes closed. She reopened them when she reached the door.

"Good afternoon. Tired, are we?" Gerald asked.

"Afternoon?" Gwen asked.

"Yes, it's one o'clock," the butler said.

"It is? I didn't realize..."

"That's quite alright, you had a long trip," he said. "The Prince has requested your presence in the ballroom."

"The ballroom? What for?"

"I've been asked not to disclose that," he whispered. "If you'd like some breakfast, I can bring you some. Otherwise, here are some clothes."

"Breakfast would be nice. And thank you." Gwen said with a yawn.

She took the clothes and closed the door. She yawned again as she placed them on the bed. She lifted the most exquisite ballgown she had ever seen. The dress was yellow like the sun, made of flowing tulle and lace. The color brought out the glow of Gwen's sun kissed skin. Gwen put it on. The sweetheart neckline accentuated her chest and hugged her waist. It had a white lace pattern over the yellow. The corset was decorated in small sparkling diamonds and white chiffon flowers. The dress flared out and spread behind her.

Snow stood on the pillow and stretched himself, looking at Gwen and meowed. He walked up to Gwen purring. She leaned down to tell Snow good morning when she heard a quiet knock on the balcony glass. She looked but didn't see anything. The knock came again. She walked over and opened the door.

"Need some help getting ready?" a female voice asked.

Gwen turned and saw Quildorra fluttering her wings.

"What are you doing here?" Gwen asked.

"I saw you through the glass and I just thought maybe you could use some help."

"That would be wonderful." Gwen smiled and walked back inside as the fairy flew in.

Glittering blue light filled the room, and all the fairies appeared.

"What are you all doing here?" Gwen asked.

"It's a surprise," Shadow said.

"A surprise? What kind of surprise?" Gwen asked.

"You'll see," a fairy with wavy red hair and lilac wings said.

"Hold still and don't move." Quildorra instructed.

Gwen stood still. The fairies fluttered and flew all around her sprinkling gold fairy dust. Studded solitaire diamond earrings appeared in Gwen's ears. The fairies' magic lifted Gwen off the ground.

"Close your eyes," a fairy told her.

Gwen closed her eyes as makeup appeared on her face. Her lips were a soft nude and earth tones shadowed her eyes. A sweet scent of freshly picked flowers filled the room.

"That smell is lovely," she said.

Gwen looked around and realized the fairies were gone.

"Shadow? Quildorra?" She called.

There was no answer. All of a sudden, golden sparkles swirled around Gwen's head and a gold tiara that spread in golden branches appeared on her head. It had small white flowers, gold butterflies, and touches of sparkling diamonds that matched her dress. Gwen lifted her dress to see bright gold lace heels. She opened the door and stepped outside.

"Ready?" the butler asked as he stood waiting.

"Yes, I am." Gwen smiled.

"Right this way," he said and escorted Gwen down the palace steps.

"I can find my way from here, thank you."

Gwen lifted her dress and carried it as she walked across the main hall and made her way past the dining room to the throne room. She approached a tall white door on the left side. She pulled it open and walked into a massive hall. The floor was covered with a carpet of pink tulips, gardenias, and orange daisies. She danced across the floor, her dress brushing over the petals as she twirled and leaped. It was the most beautiful room in all of the castle. Waiting in the middle of the room was the Prince. Gwen approached him, her dress flowing across the marble.

"Hello Gwen." He smiled at her. "May I have this dance?"

"You may," she said placing her hand in his.

He took her hand as the music began to play. Together they stepped and swayed. Gwen twirled and dipped in his arms as they danced their way across the ballroom. Gwen spun around in her dress as the sun shined down on her tiara. The Prince knelt on one knee and Gwen stopped dancing. She placed her hand in his.

"Gwen, you are the most beautiful woman I have ever seen. Since you've been here, my life has changed. You broke my curse. I've never been this happy. You are beautiful, smart, courageous, brave, but above all else– you are kind. Nothing would make me happier than for you to become my wife. Gwen, will you marry me?"

Gwen covered her mouth with her hand in disbelief. Tears filled her eyes. "Are you serious?"

"Yes, I'm serious."

"You don't think it's too soon?"

"No, of course not. You've been here for a long time now. And in that time, I've gotten to know you. I see you and I see your heart."

"Oh my god. Yes, I'll marry you."

The Prince reached into his pocket and took out a small wooden box. He held it up and opened it. The band was dainty and thin, made of pure gold. A big round diamond sat in the middle of the ring surrounded by smaller diamonds. Gwen reached out her shaking hand. The Prince took the ring from the box and slid it on her ring finger.

"Oh my god. It's so beautiful! I love it!" Gwen cried.

"And I love you, Princess Gwen. A round diamond means forever."

The Prince wrapped his arms around Gwen and embraced her. She wiped the tears from her eyes as he kissed her forehead.

As the Prince's lips met Gwen's, the sun shined brighter through the ballroom windows, casting them in a golden glow.

"I'm going to be a princess?" Gwen asked.

"You are. You're *my* princess." The Prince smiled gazing into her eyes.

"I can't wait to marry you." Gwen smiled as she held the Prince's head between her hands.

CHAPTER 17
ELIXIR KISS

For the first time in a long time, Gwen was happy. She took off her shoes and danced in the highest level of the castle's great chambers. She and the Prince would marry.

"We'll have to get you a new room," Griswald said.

"I don't mind my room. I love the balcony and the view of the sea," Gwen replied.

"That may be so but soon you'll be a princess. You'll be living up here with the Prince."

"What about Snow?"

"What about him? Do you want him to have his own room as well?" Griswald asked.

"No, of course not. Don't be silly. He's just a cat. But the hin made him a tree and he loves it."

"Ah yes, the tree. The hin really should leave crafting and building things to the other creatures. I don't know what we're going to do about that tree."

"Well maybe you can leave it alone. It's his favorite," Gwen suggested.

"Hmm, I see. Well, you will be the Princess. If you want to keep the room and have your new one in the great chambers, you can." Griswald replied.

"That would be lovely, thank you." Gwen smiled.

"Very well, you shall have both rooms," he agreed. "It's time for you to get ready for the wedding. I'll send the hin in with your dress. Let us know if you need anything."

He walked out of the room and closed the door

behind him, leaving Gwen in her new sitting room. The room was white with crystal chandeliers. Portraits framed in gold of the royal family hung on the walls between gold sconces. French furniture and floral beige rugs with petal pink flowers and light green leaves covered the floors. Gwen looked out a tall window overlooking the sea and the forests watching the beautiful summer day. The golden sun shined on her tiara and yellow dress.

Gwen sighed, was remarrying a mistake. She thought about all the heartbreak and pain she had been through. Tears filled her eyes and streamed down her face.

"Gwen, I have your dress," the bard said with delight, carrying an off-white garment bag.

Gwen wiped away her tears and turned around. "Thank you."

"Gwen, what's wrong?" Phoebe asked.

"You don't think I'm making a mistake, do you?" Gwen asked.

"What? How could you think marrying the Prince would be a mistake?"

"It's just that... I was married before to a man who didn't love me. He was so mean. He would yell, swear at me, and call me names. He wouldn't have a baby with me." The tears refilled Gwen's eyes.

"Oh Gwen, that's terrible. I'm so sorry. But I don't think you're making a mistake—not at all. I understand you were hurt. The Prince isn't that man. He hasn't hurt you, has he?" the bard asked.

"Well no," Gwen whimpered.

"Then, you have nothing to be worried about. Come, sit down," Phoebe insisted.

Gwen stepped away from the window and they sat down on a velvet tufted pink love seat.

"I'm scared." Gwen choked up as tears poured from her eyes.

"Oh Gwen, there's nothing to be scared of, I

promise. You are the only girl the Prince has ever wanted to marry. That says something, right?"

"Yeah, I guess it does." Gwen sniffled.

"It's okay to feel scared. Getting married is a big step, but the Prince loves you and I know you love him." Phoebe assured her.

"You're right." Gwen sniffled as she wiped her tears away.

"I'm your friend, Gwen. I look out for you. I will never lie to you. I'll always tell you the truth. Sometimes we have to be brave and take chances. Even the ones that scare us," Phoebe explained. "If you don't take the risk, you'll always wonder about what if and what could have been. You're nervous, it's a big day. I promise you, in all the time I've known the Prince, I've never seen him this happy."

"Are you sure?" Gwen asked.

"Of course, I'm sure. And if you didn't love the Prince, you never would have broken his curse," Phoebe said.

"You're right. I'm just...well...the unknown can be scary. Thank you, Phoebe." Gwen leaned over and hugged the bard.

"You're welcome." Phoebe smiled.

"Can you believe it? I'm getting married!" Gwen exclaimed.

"Yes, you are, and to a Prince. Gwen I'm so happy for you." The halfling smiled.

"I just can't believe this is really happening. I really am getting married," Gwen said wide eyed.

"You are. And I'll be here for you every step of the way."

"You're an amazing friend. I'm so happy that I met you." Gwen smiled.

"Now, let's get you ready. Your Prince awaits!"

Phoebe held up the bag and pulled the zipper down to reveal Gwen's dress.

"Oh my, it's so beautiful!" Gwen's eyes lit up.

Gwen reached inside and touched the material, admiring the gown. It was an off the shoulder A-line ballgown was champagne tulle and lace. It had a sweetheart neckline with touches of pearls embellished with white lace flowers and leaves. "It's perfect. Oh my god, you're gonna make me cry again," Gwen said tearing up and fanning her face with her hand.

She sat at the wardrobe table, watching herself in the mirror as she put on a pair of golden pearl earrings. The earrings had three small pearls atop a larger one. Gwen turned her head to the side. Looking back up at herself, she took a deep breath.

Then, it was time.

Snow followed her, his tail twitching as Gwen made her way to the forest. The tulle flowed brushing over the forest floor as Gwen walked. She followed a path illuminated with candles in jars. The flames danced and flickered as she passed.

She stepped down curving wooden steps. In the trees the birds chirped. She reached the final step and continued following the path. She got closer when she paused behind a tree to peek out. Her diamond halo ring sparkled as she looked out at the guests taking their seats. As she did blue sparkles filled the air. A cascading bouquet of pink peonies, baby's breath, violet hydrangeas, red roses, and willow leaves appeared in Gwen's hands. Gwen gasped as the fairies giggled.

I can't believe I'm doing this. This is real. It's actually happening, Gwen thought.

Suddenly, a strong wind ruffled the leaves. Gwen looked up as the tallest trees swayed. The shimmering golden scales of Leux flew over, circling high above. The dragon looked down with his violet-red eyes, flapped his wings, and the wizard appeared. He brushed his sleeves, cleared his throat and walked down the aisle to the front.

The clearing was filled with rows of seats made of

tree stumps with wooden boards. The aisle was decorated with moss, vines, and pillar candles burning in jars. The moss and jars sat amid the same flowers that graced Gwen's bouquet. Behind the altar was the rough tall stone of the side of a mountain with a waterfall that plunged into a rock-strewn river. The guards, knights, hobs, hin, Thomas, Griswald, Charles, the butler, and the Queen filled the seats. Bitzelsnick blinked in and turned to smile at her as he took a seat beside a hob.

Then, the Prince arrived wearing a dark brown wool suit, white dress shirt, black tie, and brown tweed vest. He walked down the aisle to meet the wizard at the end. The Prince turned and stood with his hands behind his back.

The bard rose and walked down the aisle to stand next to the Prince. Everyone quieted down and watched her walk to the altar. Phoebe lifted a violin and started to play. The music filled the forest. Gwen closed her eyes taking a deep breath as the fairies appeared. They lifted Gwen's veil and pulled it over her face. The amulet key Gwen wore began to glow.

The violin took up a new song as Snow ran to Gwen's side. Gwen smiled as the guests watched her slowly make her way down the aisle. The Prince's face lit up with a bright smile when he saw her. He wiped the corner of his eye as Gwen drew near. She held the vibrant bouquet in both hands, looking down as she approached the altar. The music slowed when Gwen looked up at the Prince. Snow walked up to the Prince and sat beside him. Phoebe stopped playing and she gently placed the violin on the ground. Gwen stepped up to the altar and Phoebe took her bouquet.

"Ladies and gentlemen, we are gathered here today to witness the love of Prince Nicholas and Gwen." Leux began.

The Queen watched from her seat, grinning in approval.

212

"I can't believe he wants to marry her. She's not worthy of being a princess," a hob groused.

"Oh, be quiet," the Queen commanded.

On the other side of the aisle, Fitz sniffled. "It seems I have something in my eye," he said wiping his eye.

Everyone watched as Snow, Gwen, and the Prince stood before the falling waterfall. The Prince took a gold wedding ring studded with diamonds and placed it on Gwen's finger. She took a gold wedding band and placed it on his. Leux held out a wooden box. Together, Nicholas and Gwen lifted the lid, and a swarm of fluttering ivory butterflies flew out.

"I now pronounce you, husband and wife. You may now kiss the bride."

Nicholas lifted Gwen's veil over her crown. They closed their eyes and kissed. The Prince lifted Gwen in the air, and they turned to face the guests.

"Ladies and gentlemen, I present to you Prince Nicholas and Princess Gwen of Sir Jericho's Kingdom," Leux announced.

Everyone stood, cheered, whistled, and applauded in celebration. Phoebe handed Gwen her bouquet. The bride and groom looked at each other and smiled. Gwen held up her bouquet as Nicholas swept her up off her feet. She grabbed her crown with one hand while she held her bouquet in the other as he carried her down the aisle.

The guests tossed handfuls of glimmering gold glitter as Nicholas ran down the aisle. Snow followed them as they ran off into the forest. As they passed an ancient oak tree, the Green Man's face appeared on the bark.

***

High in the castle's great chambers, Gwen walked across her new room to the balcony overlooking the

Fisherman Sea. Snow slept quietly in his new tree. A knock on the door startled her.

"Come in," Gwen called.

"Are you sure you want this in here? We could put it in the nursery." Haggis asked.

A very pregnant Gwen turned around to look at the halfling. She placed her hand over the top of her stomach holding it.

"Yes, I'm sure. I want her here with me at all times," she said.

"Very well then. Alright, bring it in," Haggis called over his shoulder.

He held the door open as Phoebe and Fitz carried in a white crib.

"Where do you want it?" Fitz asked.

"Over there, between the window and bookcase is fine," Gwen answered.

"The Queen has requested you meet her in the sitting room," Fitz said.

She placed her hands on her lower back as she waddled across the room.

"Here Gwen, let me help you." Phoebe rushed over and took Gwen's hand.

"Thank you," Gwen said huffing and puffing. "I think she'll be here soon."

Phoebe escorted Gwen down the hall to the sitting room and opened the door for her

"Thanks. I got it from here," Gwen said.

The Queen was standing in the middle of the room. "Gwen, there you are. How's the baby?" she asked.

"Good, she keeps kicking," Gwen answered with a sigh. "Hopefully she'll be here soon."

"Come, I have a surprise for you," the Queen said.

"A surprise?"

"Yes, come here," she said offering Gwen her hand.

They walked together over to a wall where the Queen removed a cover from one of the portraits. Gwen looked up at a painting of herself in her yellow dress, tiara, and wearing the amulet key.

"I wanted to make it official. Welcome to the family," the Queen said as she gave Gwen a hug.

"I love it. Thank you, Helena."

"You're welcome, dear. Please, have a seat," the Queen insisted.

Gwen sat in a chair looking around the room at all the portraits. There was King Jericho, Queen Helena, Prince Nicholas, and now– Princess Gwen. Snow ran into the room, jumped up on her belly and purred.

Later that day, Gwen took a stroll in the garden. Gwen paused to watch the birds splash in their baths and smell the pink roses. Suddenly, she grunted and moaned.

"Her water broke," a hob said rolling his eyes.

"I'll get someone. Be right back."

The bushes shook and leaves flew everywhere as Fitz ran through the garden pushing a wheelbarrow.

"Coming through!" he exclaimed, knocking a hob into a rose bush as he rushed over to Gwen. "I'm here. I'm here don't worry. Let's get you inside."

"Are you serious?" Gwen curled her lip and furrowed her brow at the sight of the wheelbarrow. She stood with her hands on her lower back.

"Come on, get in," Fitz told her.

"Oh boy," Gwen began her breathing exercises as she waddled around to the front of the wheelbarrow.

She cried when a pain hit her.

"Oh no, Gwen. Are you okay?" Fitz said, worried.

"I'm fine, Fitz," She assured him as she slowly sat in the wheelbarrow.

The garden filled with blue sparkles as the fairies appeared.

"Gwen, is she coming?" Shadow asked.

"Yes! Ahhhh!" Gwen said through clenched teeth.

"Hold on tight," Fitz said.

The garden door opened, and Fitz quickly took Gwen inside. "It's time!" The halfling shouted across the castle.

They got Gwen into her bed sweating. Her forehead, face, and chest glistened. The key reflected in the bright light shining in through the windows. Nicholas came to kneel by the bed and to hold Gwen's hand. Phoebe took a wet washcloth and gently blotted Gwen's forehead. A doctor came to stand at the end of the bed.

"Okay here we go," she said. "Ready? On the count of three. One...two...three... push.!"

"Ahh!" Gwen moaned, squeezing the Prince's hand.

"Oh dear!" Fitz said and fainted.

"Okay, again. Push!" the doctor said.

Gwen grunted and pushed again.

"Now one last time. Ready? Push," the doctor ordered.

Gwen whimpered in pain, released the Prince's hand, and fell back on the bed breathing heavily. The room was suddenly filled with the cries of a baby.

"You did it. We did it." Nicholas smiled.

Gwen smiled as she looked over at her husband. The doctor took the baby and walked over to a table and the fairies followed her.

"Oh, Gwen it's beautiful." Quildorra smiled.

The doctor turned around holding the baby wrapped in a pink blanket. "Congratulations, mom and dad. You have a beautiful healthy baby girl," the doctor announced. She carefully lowered the newborn into Gwen's arms.

"Well Gwen, it looks like she was the next baby girl to be born. You saved her," Phoebe said.

"What are you going to name her?" the blonde-haired doctor asked.

"Orchid, just like the flower." Gwen said with a smile.

"Hello Princess Orchid," Nicholas said.

Standing and leaning over, he reached out his finger and gently touched the baby's hand. "I'm your daddy. And this—this is your mommy."

"Hello Orchid." Gwen said. "Is Fitz okay?"

"Oh, he'll be fine," the doctor said. "Well then, I'll leave you both to it. Let me know if you need anything."

"Doctor Kate?" Gwen asked.

The doctor turned around. "Yes?"

"Thank you." Gwen smiled and looked up at her.

"Of course, now get some rest."

The days ran into months and found Gwen cradling the baby while she breastfed.

"There are my two beautiful girls!" Nicholas exclaimed when he entered the room.

He walked up to Gwen and kissed her on her forehead. He turned around doing something else. Gwen looked back down at her baby and held her close.

"Hey." Gwen said.

"Hmm?" The Prince mumbled.

"It's funny. I asked a halfling this once, but he never answered me. He actually acted quite strange... So I thought I'd ask you." Gwen paused.

The Prince turned back around and looked at Gwen.

"What ever happened to the village?" She looked up at him while holding the baby.

The Prince's eyes widened. "What makes you ask that question?"

"It's just strange that there's no village. This is a kingdom after all." She stated.

The Prince looked down at the floor and shook his head. He looked back up at his wife and took a breath.

"It's a long story," he said.

As he spoke, out in the middle of the hall behind the Prince– Gwen noticed something. It was foggy and translucent. She moved her head to get a better look. It was the apparition of the King. He levitated off the ground and drew his sword up in the air.

Gwen gasped as her eyes widened. Baby Orchid turned her head looking at the ghost and started to cry.

"What? What is it?" Nicholas asked when he turned around, but the apparition was gone.